HOPE VALLEY WAR

BROCK THOENE

THOMAS NELSON PUBLISHERS
Nashville • Atlanta • London • Vancouver

Tho

Published in association with the literary agency of Alive
Communications, 1465 Kelly Johnson Blvd. Suite #320, Colorado
Springs, CO 80920.

Published in Nashville, Tennessee, by Thomas Nelson, Inc., and dis-
tributed in Canada by Word Communications, Ltd., Richmond,
British Columbia, and in the United Kingdom by Word (UK), Ltd.,
Milton Keynes, England.

Library of Congress Cataloging-in-Publication Data

Thoene, Brock, 1952–
   Hope valley war : a novel / Brock Thoene.
     p.   cm.
   ISBN 0-7852-8071-5 (pb)
   I. Title.
PS3570.H463H66 1997
813'.54—dc20

96–30640
CIP

Printed in the United States of America

1 2 3 4 5 6 7 - 03 02 01 00 99 98 97

For our new grandbabies . . .
Jacob Chance Thoene
and
Jessica Rachel Christine McCraw
. . . with love and hope!

PROLOGUE

The faint summer breeze that rustled the curtains smelled of the pines up Schoolhouse Canyon. It was a pleasant reminder of the nearness of the forested Sierras that reared their jagged peaks a scant quarter mile behind the town of Genoa, Carson County, Utah territory. The year was 1858.

In the upstairs bedroom of the white frame home, twenty-nine-year-old Maria Thornton awoke and inhaled the soft, scented air. Her husband, William "Lucky" Thornton, lay snoring beside her. Maria pinched Lucky's elbow, and without waking he obligingly grunted and turned over. His snoring tapered off to a low rumble.

Maria shook her hair to untangle the mass of dark curls that tumbled around her head on the pillow. Settling back into the feather mattress, she was soon on the edge of sleep. Maria barely heard the owl's hoot from the snag of the locust tree, nor did she take note of an answering hoot from down the road that led toward Carson City.

What did rouse her again was the low growl that came from her dog resting on the coil rug at the foot of the bed. "What is it, Samson?" she whispered. "Bobcat up in the arroyo? Go on back to sleep."

But Samson refused to be still. He stood up with a shake and paced stiff-legged toward the bedroom door, his nails clicking on the hardwood floor. "Samson," Maria repeated with more authority, "lie down!" The dog refused to obey and whined as he scratched at the panel.

Maria glanced at her husband. He was still sound asleep. Best to let him rest, she thought. There had been nothing but trying days of late. Whatever it was, she and Samson could handle it. She felt no fear of robbers, for the Thorntons had nothing of value to steal. Nor was she concerned about attack by Washoe Indians, with whom they were on friendly terms. "A skunk after some eggs again," she muttered to Samson as she drew a robe on over her cotton nightgown. "You can chase him off, but you'll sleep outside after!"

Samson bustled past her down the steps toward the front door. The staircase was dark, but Maria lit no lamp as she descended. She guided herself by one hand on the oak banister. When she reached the bottom she spared a quick look at the entrance to the guest bedroom where her husband's younger brother, nineteen-year-old Kit, was sleeping along with her only child, George, age nine.

Apparently they had not awakened either. Maria smiled at the uselessness of menfolk.

Beside the front door she paused, one hand on the brass knob. The dog was whining eagerly to get at whatever was out there. Was there any cause for alarm? In the deepest part of the previous winter, a mountain lion had been driven by the deep snows to seek easier prey in the valley below. The cougar had raided three ranches, killing calves and sheep, before being shot. This was June, but caution might still be wise. Maria recrossed the front room and took down the loaded double-barrel shotgun from above the mantle. For a girl who had come of age in the mining camps of the California Gold Rush, grasping the stock of the weapon and checking to see that the percussion caps were in place came naturally.

"All right, Samson," she declared, "I'm ready." Maria flung open the door and the dog dashed out, leaping off the porch and charging around the corner of the house. The barn! She had been right all along. Some nocturnal prowling critter was after the henhouse. Maria could hear Samson's growls and sharp yelps tracing the path toward the stable.

Cradling the shotgun across her chest, Maria turned in the doorway to reach up for the lantern hanging there when the dog's barking ceased abruptly. "Samson?" she called. She fumbled in the pocket of her robe for the matches.

A hand shot out of the darkness and grabbed the barrel of the shotgun, wrenching it from her. At the same instant, another hand clamped across her mouth, stifling the scream that jumped into her throat. Her eyes grew wide with terror at the apparition that confronted her: a figure dressed all in black with a grotesque scarecrow's face dragged her out of the doorway, flung her cheek first against the living room window, and held her there. "Keep her here!" her assailant commanded. "Now move! Move!" the creature hissed. "Upstairs!" A different set of rough hands pressed Maria against the window, but the exchange was not made without a squeak of warning escaping from her mouth.

Through the wavy pane of glass, Maria saw a half dozen similarly dressed forms hurry out of the night and into her home. When three of the men had dashed up the stairs, the downstairs bedroom door was flung open and Kit appeared. "Maria?" he called. "Keep back, George! What's all the . . . ?" He never completed his question as two hooded forms jumped him. Kit fought back, landing a punch that staggered one of his attackers, then a pistol barrel clapped him alongside his left ear, and he slid down to the floor.

Maria could hear the upstairs bedroom door kick open, and there was a roar of gunfire. The scene on the landing was both illuminated and frozen in the muzzle blast. The foremost intruder fell backward, clutching his arm and swearing.

From a place of concealment beside the fireplace, the leader of the attackers ordered, "Lucky Thornton! Give yourself up!" Another gunshot from Lucky's .44 replied to this decree, tearing a furrow in the oak planks.

"We've got your wife and brother," the hoarse voice of the commander asserted. "Throw your gun out and come peaceable, and they won't get hurt."

There was a moment's silence and then the heavy-framed Colt bounced on the landing and thumped to the floor.

The ringleader of the mob struck a match and lit an oil lamp. By its smoky yellow glow, Maria saw her husband, closely guarded by two men with six shooters, come slowly down the stairs. Lucky wore only a long white nightshirt, and the pale shroud of the man's dress matched the ashen hue of his face. The contrast between her husband's pallor and the evil black garb of the intruders was riveting. Maria wanted to scream; wanted to demand, "What are you doing to him? What is this? Who are you?" but none of these outcries would pass her lips.

Instead she watched with paralyzed dread as her husband was escorted across the front room toward the door. As Lucky drew even with his son's room, George darted out of the shadows to grab his father around the waist. "Don't go!" he cried. "Don't go with them!"

One of the marauders seized the boy roughly by the shoulders and jerked him away, but the leader of the group intervened. "Leave 'em be a minute," he said tersely. Then to Lucky he added, "Tell him not to try and follow us."

Maria saw her husband stoop to the boy's height. "Be strong," he said. "Thorntons are tough. Stay with your mother and take care of her. Understand?"

George wiped away a tear with the back of one hand and nodded his agreement without speaking.

"Go to your mother then," Lucky said, gesturing toward the window. George ran to his mother's side.

"What about him?" one of the nightriders growled, pointing toward Kit, who still lay unconscious on the floor. "He ain't tied up . . . or dead." The phrase ended on a suggestive note.

"Let him alone," the commander ordered. "He won't be awake soon enough to bother us. Tell your wife not to follow nor try to set anyone else on our track," he repeated to Lucky. "We don't want anyone else to get hurt; that's not our intent."

Maria's knees buckled at the import of the words "anyone else." She sagged toward the window and put her hand on the shoulder of her son to steady herself.

The band of raiders had reached the doorway with their prisoner. "Tie his hands behind him," the chief said.

"Wait, for God's sake, just a moment more," Lucky pleaded, showing the first sign of emotion.

The scarecrow's head nodded once. "Make it quick." The leader gave a shrill whistle into the night that was replied to from the grove of scrub oak up in the draw.

Lucky folded Maria in his arms. George pressed close against them both. "Good-bye," Lucky said simply. "I love you. You are the best wife a man could ever want."

They tied his hands and hobbled his ankles so he could not run. Then they led him away down the steps and toward the sound of approaching horses.

When they had gone, Maria stumbled back into the house and sat sobbing on the floor. She cradled the broken head of her brother-in-law while George obeyed her gasped instructions to fetch water and bandages.

Lucky Thornton lay in the wagonbed of his captors, trussed like a Christmas goose. The unmatched team of one brown mule and one white mule that drew the rig were alike in the way they rolled their eyes at the masked figures on horseback flanking them. They started and jerked at every bat and nightjar that flew, making the driver swear and saw at the leads to keep them from jumping the ditch beside the road.

The cavalcade headed north, away from Genoa and away from any hope of rescue by Thornton's friends. There was no undue haste among the raiders. They were unafraid of any interruption of their work. The troop followed the northward bend of the Carson River till reaching the junction of Clear Creek, then turned aside.

Lucky Thornton knew exactly where he was and where they were taking him long before the troop pulled through the gates of Manny Penrod's ranch. The nightriders had chosen well; the barn was in the center of flat acreage and pasture land that extended for miles in every direction. If anyone mounted a rescue attempt, they would be spotted a long ways off.

Two of the guards spurred ahead and opened the passage into the barn so the wagon could be driven directly inside. Only after all were in and the doors closed again were lanterns lit, and Thornton's abductors removed their masks.

He knew them all. Some were open enemies like Major Frey and the gambler, Bernard King. Others were respectable townspeople captive in some way to Frey's power, like Curtis Raycraft, who owned the livery, and rancher Manny Penrod. There was even one whom Lucky had thought a friend: Lute Olds. Then there was Rough Elliott: a saloon tough hired to do an unpleasant job without any troubling pangs of conscience.

"Take off the gag," ordered the leader, "and untie his legs so he can stand. We need to proceed with the trial."

Thornton fixed his eyes on those of his chief opponent. As soon as he could speak he said, "Let it alone, Frey. What's the point of playing charades, when everyone including me knows what's to be? The only thing you'll hear from me is that none of you will get away with this."

Frey ignored the gibe. "Lucky Thornton, you stand accused of conspiring with the criminal Amon Edwards to rob and murder the rancher François Gordier. How do you plead?"

Getting into an argument about this mockery of a trial was pointless. Thornton occupied his time looking from face to face among his captors, searching for any hint of mercy or weakness to which he could appeal. The lantern light within the dusty cavern of the barn exposed only the pitiless countenances of his enemies and the fixedly downcast stares of the others.

The Major droned on about Edwards and Gordier, about Hope Valley, about cattle rustling and homicide, weaving a concocted tale of justification for what was to come. Major Frey sounded as though he had even convinced himself that this night's business was completely honorable and just.

Amongst all the bearded faces of the Major's cronies and hired thugs, the pale yellow glow from the single lamp fell on only one unshaven cheek. Thornton squinted his eyes and contorted his body, trying to peer around a post and into the gloom at the boyish features of one not much different in age from his own brother Kit.

The young man saw Thornton's gaze light on him and dropped his own face to the straw-covered dirt floor. Thornton continued to stare at the boy, silently urging him to raise his eyes again. Unwilling, yet unable to resist, the young man did so, like a kangaroo rat transfixed by the stare of a sidewinder. Thornton recognized him then: the Major's own son, Lawrence Frey, eighteen years old.

The Major was getting his money's worth from the bought-and-paid-for witnesses. "You were seen in the company of Amon Edwards one day before Gordier was found brutally murdered with an ax. Your conversation was overheard as you conspired to cause Gordier's death," the Major summarized.

"Give it up!" Lucky interrupted at last. "On the day before Gordier was killed, I was on the other side of the mountains, clear up at Bone's Toll Station. Mister Thick, who runs the station, will verify this. A little more attention to detail, if you please."

"By gad, sir," erupted Manny Penrod, "have you no sense of the seriousness of this occasion?"

"My sense," replied Thornton with a sneer, "is that you mean to hang me in cold blood for no proven wrongdoing whatsoever. My death, ordered by this caricature of a court, is to satisfy the greed of all of you and the ambition of the Major at whose trough you all feed. Serious, sir? Deadly serious, but ludicrous for all that! Where is Edwards who is accused with me? Where are the witnesses who can establish my innocence in this matter? What about Thick? He is my alibi, but will you be allowed to hear from him? No sir, you will not!"

Lucky's remarks were directed toward Penrod, the balding man with the graying beard and mustache, but he was intent on observing the reaction of young Frey. Suddenly Lucky spoke directly to the boy. "Run, Lawrence! Get Constable Denton! Don't have my blood on your conscience! Make them call Thick. He'll clear me!"

"Don't move, Lawrence!" Frey ordered. The Major laid a restraining hand on his son's arm. The teenager grew even more pale, but he raised no objection. "And pay no heed to his lies. Mister Thick is the very man who has testified that he saw Thornton with Edwards!"

The burlesque hearing wound to its conclusion. The Major, in his best judicial manner, intoned, "You have heard the evidence. What says the jury?"

"Guilty," snapped Rough Elliott before anyone else could speak. A chorus of guilty verdicts concurred. Some were loud and firmly spoken, like Bernard King's and Major Frey's. Others were mumbled and doubtful, as uttered by Curtis Raycraft, Manny Penrod, and Lute Olds, but in the end, no one disagreed, though Lawrence Frey's voice could not be heard at all.

"Sentence to be carried out immediately," declared the Major. "And we here, constituting this lawful court, all agree to the justice of the sentence and do hereby bind ourselves on pain of death to never reveal the identities of any of the members of this body nor to speak of this night's particulars."

Thornton snorted again, wondering if he was the only person in the room who saw the irony behind secret justice and coerced silence. Lawrence Frey was trembling, visibly shaking. He looked as though he might bolt into the sagebrush at any moment.

Rough Elliott, with his wirebrush beard and potato-shaped nose, noticed also. "What about him?" he growled, jerking a thumb at young Frey. "He don't look steady."

"He'll stick," said the Major. "Won't you, Lawrence?" The boy snapped his head downward sharply to show his agreement.

There was a whispered conference between the Major and Elliott, then the Major made an announcement. "We'll draw straws to see who drives the team," he said. "I'll draw first, then each man in the room until the short is drawn. Go on now, get it done."

Four men took their wisp of hay and then it was young Frey's turn. He pulled out a twig half the length of the others and stepped back with a look of horror on his face. "What? What's this mean?" he gasped.

"Means you're the executioner, sonny. Get up on that box." Lawrence extended his hands in protest and tried to back away, but Elliott caught him by the arm and yanked him forward. "The duty's yourn. Get goin'."

A coil of hemp was flung over a beam and a noose formed on the end to dangle in front of Thornton's face. He did not wait to be manhandled into position, but thrust his head into the loop. "I'm better than any of you," he said. "And since you mean to hang me, I won't die like a hog!" Lawrence Frey sat with the reins dangling limply from his bloodless fingers, and tears gathered in his eyes. "They didn't steal your humanity either, boy," Thornton said. "Don't be afraid; whip 'em up sharp and get it done."

A moment later, Lucky Thornton's string of luck had all run out.

CHAPTER 1

It was near the end of the Fall gather, and we were pushing cattle down from the high feed of Tobias meadows toward the lower Carver Pastures. It was a sleepy afternoon, and my horse, Shad, was doing most of the work. I was riding easy when Stoney Brooks came charging up the Frog Creek Trail like a whole tribe of Comanches was after him. His buckskin leggings were flapping, and his bay was lathered. Since there were no hostile Indians in near four-hundred miles any direction, my first thought was that he was racing somebody, on a bet probably. Stoney had been below, to Glennville, to pick up some salt and coffee that Cookie wanted.

My next thought was that it was a good thing the ramrod, Abner Slater, was nowhere about to see Stoney's uphill gallop. You could break your own neck doing any fool thing you pleased, but damage Bar C stock to no purpose, and Slater would wrench your head off and hand it to you.

Stoney spotted me up in the rocks where I was hazing a cow and a late-born calf out of a gooseberry tangle. He gave a whoop and a holler and spurred straight across a shaley place that a sane man would not have walked his mount over. "John," he yelled, reaching inside his leather jacket and waving a paper. "You got a letter! Look here! A letter!"

Such a life in the cow camps that a little thing like a letter could raise such a fuss. Still, I had to admit that my own heart jumped up a notch in rhythm. Who would be writing me, unless it was bad news? My own people were far away, back East for the most part. For anyone to bother writing must mean trouble.

"And lookee," Stoney cackled. "It's from a female too!" He yanked his panting, jug-headed horse to a stop on the ledge, scaring the calf and its mama. They plunged back into the thickest part of the scrub from which I had been working near an hour to extract them.

"Give me that," I said, leaning across and snatching the letter out of his hand. Stoney perched there with a stupid grin on his freckled face, and I knew he was not going anywhere until I had shared the news, good or bad. At least he had not been fooling me; the paper had my name, John Thornton, written plain as anything.

Despite Stoney's impatience, I sat for a spell holding the letter in my hand, studying the outside and thinking. From the date on the front it had taken near three months to get to me. The original address on the pale blue envelope was in Maria's elegant hand; I knew it right off. I also recognized the faint lavender scent that still clung to the paper despite a number of greasy finger smudges and nose prints from appreciative letter carriers.

She had recalled that I once owned a share of a mine in Downieville and had tried me there first. It tickled me to think she remembered.

But I had long since moved on from Downieville. Drifting south in search of that elusive big strike and the even more elusive ease for my soul, I had gone on to Coarsegold. The letter had properly tried to follow me there. But after arriving sometime behind my departure, it had unaccountably gone off to the old Spanish mission town of San Luis Obispo, while I had actually crossed the Sierras to the upper Kern River.

After a time I opened the envelope as carefully as my big, callused hands would permit and unfolded the single sheet inside. I could feel my face get warm when I read her greeting, just as if she stood right in front of me.

Then, an instant later, I caught my breath, and my skin grew icy cold. "What?" Stoney asked. "What is it? I ain't seen your map this set in granite since you caught them drunks roughin' up that Yokut squaw."

I read the first two lines again, just to make sure there was no mistake. *John*, it said. *I need your help. Lucky has been lynched.* She went on to explain what had happened and so forth, but all that mattered to me was this: My brother was dead and Maria had asked for me.

"Hey!" boomed the whiskey-roughened voice of Abner Slater from the next ridge over. "Mister Carver don't pay riders to have no tea parties. Light a shuck under you both, and shift them cows."

Stoney pricked his nag so sharply with his spurs that it almost jumped sideways off the ledge. "Let's get goin'," he muttered in a guilty tone, "double quick."

When I did not move fast enough to suit him, Slater yelled again. "You hear me, John Thornton? Shake it up or you're through." I was thinking hard. Then I carefully folded the letter and tucked it into my shirt.

"Come on," Stoney urged. "He sounds mad enough to swallow a horned toad backwards." Then in a syrupy voice, he said loud enough for Slater to hear, "Right away, Mister Slater."

Directly I nudged Shad into a lope away from the cows and toward the ramrod. I heard Stoney yell something to me, but I paid him no mind.

"What do you want, Thornton?" Slater grumbled. "Didn't I tell you to get back to work?"

"I'm leaving," I said, simple as that. Slater looked dumbfounded. "Today. You know this is my horse and my rig. Nothing I have here but what's my own. I'll leave an address with the home ranch where you can send my time." And with that I was gone, heading back north toward Utah territory, Maria, and God only knew what kind of trouble.

It took me the better part of a week to make the journey from the southern Sierras to the Mother Lode country.

They were my worst seven days in many a year, what with fretting about Maria. The Pioneer stages covered the same distance in thirty-five hours, making my pace all the more painful. But having neither enough money for coach fare, nor wanting to kill Shad, I had to take it slower.

We traveled the main highways as far as Placerville and then followed the stage route over the Carson Pass and down the eastern slope through Hope Valley. When I got even with Snowshoe Thompson's place at Diamond Springs, I reined Shad aside and reflected once more on what I was riding into.

I stood in need of more information than was contained in Maria's letter. A hundred days had already gone by since she penned those lines. What direction was the wind blowing now?

Snowshoe was the man to ask for news right enough. The long-bearded Norwegian carried the mail across the mountains between the American River diggings and the Washoe mines. Being much in demand and genial with all, he heard everything within a fifty-mile radius and was free with what he heard. And if we had not been especially close in the old days, he bore me no ill will that I knew.

Unfortunately, there was no one about at the Thompson cabin, so I had to press on no wiser than before. It had been years since I was last in those parts, and it was unlikely that many folks thereabouts could call me to mind. Still, a man has to be a fool to walk into a rattlesnake's den in his bare feet. It seemed best to me to go quietly straight to the ranch before anyone with unfriendly notions found out there was another Thornton about.

With that in mind, when we came to the fork, Shad and I followed the deserted path called the Old Emigrant Trail where it skirted the valley of the Carson until we reached a hillside above my brother's ranch. Or rather, his widow's place, I reminded myself.

It was just at dawn, and I sat for a spell beneath a jack pine that stood sentinel on the knoll overlooking the spread called the Lucky T. A blue jay scolded me from the branches over my head, chattering about my being where I did not belong. No one paid him any heed however, and all was quiet below me. A lamp came to life in the downstairs sitting room and a wisp of smoke curled lazily upward from the kitchen chimney. Peaceful enough it was, without a danger in sight.

When Shad and I eased into the yard by way of the back pasture, it seemed to me that some things had changed after all. There was an air of disrepair about the place. The barn stood in need of a coat of whitewash, the garden was overgrown with weeds, and a buggy with a busted seat was hoisted off the ground on a pair of barrels. It was grit-covered, as if it had been awaiting repair a long while already. When Lucky was alive he would never have tolerated such shabbiness, meaning Maria would never have permitted it.

It would not do to present myself at the kitchen door like a saddle tramp hunting a meal, though that description fit me better than most. Still, I was family, so brushing the road dust off myself as best I could, I tied Shad to the rail beside the front porch and climbed the steps. Even before raising my knuckles to knock, I thought I caught a glimpse of a face sneaking a look at me through a window, but it darted back quick as I turned.

Knowing that folks were about made me bold to knock the third time when no one answered my first two raps. If I had been expecting a warm reception and an embrace of welcome, I had sure been singing from the wrong hymnal. The door, when it finally opened, parted a crack barely wide enough to let a cat through.

The dark eye that regarded me through the slit was unfriendly, suspicious, and fearful all at once. It also belonged to nobody I recognized. "What do you want?" a reedy voice inquired in an anxious way that confirmed all I had guessed from appearances.

"'Scuse me," I said, polite enough. "Isn't this the Thornton place? I'm trying to find Maria Thornton."

"There's no one here by that name. This is our place. You just get on out of here!" The words of what I judged to be a late adolescent boy rose to an almost frantic pitch for no reason I could see.

"Now look here, sonny, I don't mean to cause any trouble," I said, holding my hands up. But just then he started to close the door in my face, and I will admit to getting a touch riled. I shot my boot forward and wedged the toe between the panel and the frame. "No trouble,"

I repeated as the boy's face grew even more wild looking, "but I do need an answer to my question."

"She ain't here!" he repeated forcefully. "Now I told you to go! Get away!"

There was much more going on here than just a lack of neighborliness. This green sprout seemed positively panicked at my inquiry, scared as if he'd seen a ghost.

Before I could even raise the issue of Maria's whereabouts again, a woman's voice, shrill and unpleasant as a crosscut saw hitting a rock, yelled from across the room, "Lawrence, who is that? What's he want?"

The door that had been held closed to the width of my foot was now flung widely open. It revealed a woman of about forty, lean and careworn, as if her two score years had cost her three score in grief and toil.

"What do you want here? What's this all about?" She roughly shoved aside the youth I guessed to be her son and by sheer force of will backed me up a pace. She appeared to be of the belief that you can win any argument by never letting your opponent speak at all. "Whatever you're selling, we don't want any. Now go on before I sic the dogs on you."

It seemed that the quiet, easy approach was not producing helpful results. Just that quickly I threw away my resolve to keep my identity secret. I guess I hoped to startle them into some response. "I'm not selling anything," I remarked real fast in the split second when the woman paused to draw breath. "I'm John Thornton, brother of Lucky, who used to own this place. I'm searching for his widow."

The boy's face showed a strange mix of worry and relief, almost as if my words had lifted one burden and left another in its place. His ma narrowed her eyes and gazed away up toward her mousy brown hair like she was hunting cobwebs in the corner of the doorframe. I knew from her expression she was searching for the right lie to tell me. "This is the Frey place now. We own it," she said. "My husband bought it. We don't know anything about any other owner nor this woman, whoever she is. Now get along. We don't want strangers here."

"Well now, ma'am, maybe I could just wait and speak with your husband when he gets home," I said reasonably.

"You will not!" she snapped, stamping her foot on the floor. "Lawrence, get the dogs! And call Rough Elliott to get up here . . . tell him to bring his gun."

"No need for that," I said, making gentling motions with my hands as I backed down the porch. "What's your husband's name so's I can ask for him in town?"

"Get the dogs!"

As the boy darted past me and around the corner, I tipped my hat politely and said I'd call again some other day. Then Shad and I trotted off toward Genoa.

Genoa, pronounced for some unknown reason with the accent on the second syllable, had grown up since I saw it last. Back when I was prospecting in those parts, the community that nestled in a crook at the base of the Sierras had been called Mormon Station, on account of being the westward-most outpost of Brigham Young's empire. In fact, he had ordered families to move there in large numbers, so as to guarantee a faithful voting population when it came to selecting judges and so forth.

No more at first then a stockade and a trading post on the Emigrant Trail, the town had been renamed after it prospered enough to be selected the county seat of Carson County back in 1855.

Shad and I attracted no particular notice as we rode into town on Main Street. I reined in at Raycraft's Livery and flipped the stableboy a nickel to feed, water, and curry the bay. Then I sauntered in a casual way down the boardwalk past the Masonic Lodge, the Gomez barbershop, and Manny Penrod's smithy.

From the corner outside the blacksmith's, I could study a hotel with the name Frey displayed over the door and had a clear view both directions up and down the street. I stood there wondering where to make my first call and waiting to see if something would happen to give me a clue. I did not have long to wait.

Before five minutes had passed, thundering into town came that same kid I had seen out at the ranch. He was accompanied by an evil-looking cuss that I took to be Rough Elliott, the ranch hand the boy's mother had been hollering for.

I pulled the brim of my hat down over my eyes and leaned back in the corner where the brick front of the

Mason's building stuck out past the barbershop. The man and the boy split up almost right in front of me, with the hard case trotting his wiry-looking buckskin over toward the courthouse.

The boy, Lawrence, as I had heard him called, first went into the hotel, but he came back out a minute later and headed on a slant across the highway as if coming right for me. He did not see me, though, and popped into the barbershop.

I leaned out from my spot and moved just enough to where I could hear what passed inside the tonsorial parlor. "Major," I heard him address a big fellow sitting in the chair while the barber stropped a straight razor. The man's neck below his coal-black beard was already lathered.

"What's wrong, Lawrence? You look like you've seen a ghost."

"Yessir," the boy stuttered. "That is, someone's been asking after Missus Thornton, and Ma told me to find you pronto." What can be said about a man who made his own son call him Major?

"Why all the fuss? We bought the place fair and square. Why didn't you just tell the party she sold the ranch and moved away?"

"I tried to, but he wouldn't leave," the kid protested.

"Pay it no mind," the burly man in the chair said. "It doesn't signify."

"But he said his name was Thornton too . . . John Thornton!"

That distinguished-looking gentleman almost cut his own throat, so fast did he sit bolt upright under the razor. Pushing the barber's arm aside, he demanded, "What'd he look like, this Thornton? What'd you tell him? Where'd he go?"

Lawrence saw that he'd gotten his father's attention, and now he was not at all sure he wanted it. "I don't know where he went. He just asked after Maria Thornton, and then he rode off. He was a big man, better'n six feet and a couple hundred pounds, I guess. Older looking than . . . than . . ." Here the boy ran out of words, but I guessed he was comparing my looks to my younger brother's. His next words confirmed the thought. "When he first come up to the door, I thought it was Lucky alive again," Lawrence squeaked.

"That is not possible," asserted Major Frey with the confidence of one who knew something beyond a doubt. He scrubbed the lather from his neck and tossed the towel on the floor. "Come along, Lawrence," he ordered brusquely. "Let's go over to the Courthouse."

"Yessir," Lawrence agreed. "Rough Elliott is already down there looking for you."

As he and the boy made for the door, I quickly sunk back in the shadows and bent over to straighten my chaps. Once outside they turned away from me toward the brick building at the other end of town without so much as a glance my way.

I was filing away names and descriptions for later use. There was much unexplained here, but my first goal was still to locate Maria, so I made no move toward confrontation just then.

Directly across the street from me was J. R. Terwilliger's General Store. It looked like as good a spot as any to continue my research, even if I had no expectation of actually speaking with the proprietor. Terwilliger had been as old as the Sierras when I knew him back in the earlies, and I imagined that he had long since gone to his reward.

That just shows what jumping to conclusions can do. I opened the door to the center aisle of a store that smelled of oiled harness leather and roasting coffee beans. As soon as the bell jingled, Twilly poked his knot of frizzy white hair out from behind a stack of blankets on the counter, as he was too short to see over the top.

Scrawny and with a bird-like conversational habit of hopping from one topic to another, Twilly looked and sounded like a woodpecker. "'Lo, John," he said sprightly. "Been expecting you. I knew you'd be back when you heard the news. Ever strike the big bonanza? You've aged some . . . more'n some."

Twilly had always made more money in one day selling camp goods to me and other prospectors than I ever saw in a month of panning for flakes in icy streams. "No," I said with a grin. "But you, you old coot, don't look one day older than ever."

"Clean living," Twilly said, slapping together his bony hands in front of his fence-post sized chest. "It was a bad business, John, bad."

I gathered from this shift that he was referring to what

happened to my brother. A fella had to be nimble-witted to keep up with Twilly. "Tell me what happened."

His eyes widened, and he clapped a hand over his mouth like he'd said too much already. "I don't know anything," he maintained. "Best you ride on, John. You'll only get in trouble if you stay around."

"What about the ranch? Where's Maria, Twilly? And the child?"

"You been down in Spanish Californy, John? What do they think of President Buchanan over there? Folks say he's too soft on the slavery question. Just wants to get along any old way."

"Maria," I said again. "At least tell me where she went." But Twilly, contrary to a lifetime habit, refused to say more. "What are you scared of, Twilly?"

"Not now, John, not now," he begged. "I . . ."

The doorchime jingled again, and the big plug-ugly known as Rough Elliott walked in. When he saw me his chin went up, and his hand dropped toward the gun butt that protruded from his pants pocket. I could see from the look on his face that he figured me for the one he had been searching for, but he was not entirely certain. "All right, Twilly," I said. "I'm going now. See you later." Elliott and I kept our eyes locked on each other, though neither of us spoke. Even after I passed him, I could feel his stare on the back of my head.

Not having any desire to cause Twilly any trouble, I walked in front of the shop window like I was heading for the hotel. But quick as I came to the alley between

Terwilliger's and Olds's Meat Market, I ducked down it and circled the back of the General Store. I knew the layout from the old days; Twilly lived in a pair of rooms at the way back, then the stock room was in the middle of the building with a curtained entrance into the store proper.

The backdoor opened with barely a squeak, and I tiptoed across his kitchen and put my ear up to the drape. "Was that John Thornton?" I heard Elliott demand. "Answer me, you old sack of bones."

"I don't know any John Thornton," Twilly protested. His denial ended with a strangled croak, and there was the sound of leather scraping across something.

Peeking through the gap in the cloth partition, I saw Rough Elliott grab Twilly by the arms and hoist the little man up. Twilly's boot toes drug on the counter, knocking the blankets every direction and busting a jar of stick candy on the floor.

"We'll see how much you remember when I poke your face in the lye pot," Elliott laughed. He spun Twilly around in his arms like a child, and held him head downward. Twilly was shrieking, but he was squeezed so tight that only a frantic squeal like an injured rabbit makes came out. Elliott kicked the clay lid off the crock, exposing the caustic chemical just a foot below Twilly's jaw. "Was that Thornton?" the cutthroat demanded. "What did you say to him? Tell me, or I'll burn your eyes out!"

I jumped through the curtain and grabbed up the first thing that came to hand, which was a keg of nails. As I had guessed, the noise I made caused Elliott to spin around, still holding Terwilliger. I shouted, "Here, catch," and flung the fifty pound drum hard as I could.

Rough Elliott did real well. He dropped Twilly like a flash and almost got his hands up to catch the keg. He did manage to keep it from bashing him in the chest, but his sudden move deflected the barrel upward to strike him in the chin. The keg shattered in his face and he stumbled backwards over the lye crock. When he hit the floor, he was out cold.

"Thanks, John," Twilly managed, gingerly flapping his skinny arms around his ribs to see if any were busted.

"I'm not so different from him," I warned. "I want answers too."

Twilly looked Elliott over to see if the man was really unconscious, such was the terror this ape inspired in defenseless folks. Then Twilly said, "He works for the Freys. Maria lives in the old sawmill cook shack. I swear that's all I know, John."

"All right, Twilly," I said at last. "I'll drag this carcass out into the street, and you lock up."

"What are you gonna do with him?"

"Drop him beside the horse trough," I said. "He'll thank me when he comes to and feels that lye he fell in eating through his britches."

CHAPTER 2

I felt the eyes of all of Genoa on me as I mounted Shad and lit out toward the mountains and Lucky's sawmill.

It was still early afternoon, but the sun had moved west of the craggy Sierras and my path was all in shadow. It was plain from the condition of the road that it had been a long while since Lucky's lumber carts had passed this way. The deep ruts carved by the iron rims of the freight wagons were rounded from last season's rain. The packed earth bore the recent hoof marks of two shod horses and a clutter of smaller tracks made from a half dozen shoeless pack burros.

What had happened to the thriving sawmill business? It was clear that the town of Genoa was still growing. I recalled the sound of hammers and the frames of three new structures on Main Street that very morning. It had not occurred to me to ask where the stacks of fresh-cut lumber had come from. When Twilly explained that Maria and the boy were staying out at the sawmill, I figured she had taken over Lucky's business. The derelict road told a different tale.

I reined up on a rise and turned to look down on the distant, sunlit buildings of Genoa. A quail called a warning to his fellows from a clump of manzanita. A gray-backed lizard skittered across a boulder on the slope beneath me. Soft wind rattled the dry autumn sagebrush then rushed through the pine trees on the high slopes with a sound like water.

Peaceful, I thought. Peaceful as death. Gazing at the dusty trail, I shuddered as Lucky's face came clear to my mind. It was in this very place I had last seen him alive. He had been driving a six-up team pulling a wagonload of planks down to the valley. My team. My wagon. My lumber. He was smiling because I had lost everything to him. I had lost Maria.

Strange how his grin was branded on my memory. The image of him slapping the reins down hard on the backs of the horses sent a wave of renewed anger through me.

He bade me farewell with a light, laughing voice.

"You always were a fool, John! But you were right from the start. We can't share everything," he called as the wagon rumbled past me. "The lumbermill? The ranch? Small potatoes. We might have stayed partners in all that except for Maria. Can't share her, can we brother? She loves me, you know. Winner takes all. That's what we agreed. Whilst I'm alive I won't have you looking at her like you do. Now gather your gear and clear out."

I could have killed my brother easily that day. Instead I had stopped at the sawmill long enough to pack then rode on up the spine of the mountain to where the waters of the great Tahoe sparkled. For a month I had camped beside the lake and considered committing the sin of Cain against my brother.

Then news from Genoa came to me by way of an old placer miner named Smike who stopped at my camp near supper time. Miss Maria Foquette had married Lucky Thornton only four days after I left Genoa. Over beans and bacon the grizzled relic told me about the wedding and the big feed that Lucky put on for the entire town. A right handsome couple were Maria and Lucky. The bride looked at the bridegroom with such adoration that it made even the toughest men in Genoa weep.

With Smike's recitation of the event, I knew it was Lucky she loved, not me. Lucky was right. A sawmill and a ranch were small potatoes compared to her.

I gave up my thoughts of vengeance that very night. Next morning I broke camp and rode on. For nine years I carried the bitterness of that day with me. Hatred was the only thing I kept from all my memories of Lucky. I held on to it when I had nothing else. I rehearsed it in my mind late nights at a campfire, substituted his form when I killed coyotes.

"Whilst I'm alive . . ." Lucky had said to me at our parting.

How often in the long seasons that followed had I wished him dead?

Now it was done. Someone else's hand had shed his blood, but I had wished it so. It was true that Lucky had a way of making enemies out of the best of friends. I was not surprised that someone had murdered him. Nor was I surprised at the manner in which he had been killed.

What surprised me was that all my anger toward him suddenly turned to regret. The memories of happy times we had spent together flooded over me. I thought of the son he left behind. I thought of our mother and father and our boyhood in the hills of New York. For the first time since our harsh farewell nine years before I felt the loss of my brother. Good-bye was hard after all.

All this came to me clearly as I looked down at the shifting shadows of the Carson Valley.

A steep, treacherous trail branched off from the broader path of Sawmill Road. It cut a swath straight up through the long switchbacks and would save a full hour on the journey. But it was not the consideration of time that caused me to turn from the easier track. When I left Genoa, the feeling came strong upon me that I was being followed. The wagon road was wide open. A lone rider made a stark target against the backdrop of the hillside. A crack shot with a Sharps .52 rifle and a clear view could turn me to crow bait before I spotted him.

Experience had taught me that only a fool would skyline himself. I did not intend to become anybody's fool. That afternoon I felt something like a deer must feel when a mountain lion is hungry and on the prowl. I had yet to see the face of the lion who stalked me, but I knew he was lurking there just the same.

I glanced up at the narrow track, and trusting that Shad would find footing, I gave the horse his head. Shad was a mountain-bred pony, and he took to the ledge with ease. Picking his way between boulders and moving carefully over loose shale and crumbling granite, he seemed unperturbed as we rose a thousand feet and more above the floor of the canyon. As for myself, I never much cared to be anyplace higher than my own head. I just leaned into his shoulders to make his burden lighter and tried not to look down. I cussed and prayed in alternate breaths.

From the opposite cliff, a golden eagle leapt from the rim of her large nest and glided downward to fly past me at eye level. With a piercing cry, she circled once as a warning that I was an intruder in her world. I heard the swish of her wings upon the updraft as she soared effortlessly back to her chicks.

For thirty minutes the gelding climbed steadily, coming at last to where Sawmill Road emptied onto a gently sloping meadow. Lucky and I had carved out the track and built the sawmill ten years before. A half mile wide and a mile deep, the bench of thin soil over granite was overshadowed by a range of peaks at the westerly end. I could clearly see the spindly frame of the old flume rising up from the red painted shingles of the sawmill. Silhouetted against the boulder strewn hillside, a section of the flume was broken, and a steady stream of water flowed from it.

My first thought was that I would have to mend the flume. Then it came to me that last time I had been here, the place had been alive with the ear-splitting noise of the lumber business—the buzz of saw against wood, the shouts of teamsters, and the clatter of iron wheels.

Today the mill was silent. Stacks of weathered planks were in the yard as if waiting for wagons that never came. Uncut logs lay rotting beside the main building. More than the flume needed mending.

What had happened here, I wondered as I stared up at the bullet-riddled sign which still read THORNTON BROTHERS. The only hint of life was a crooked finger of woodsmoke pointing skyward from the cook shack stovepipe. My heart beat a little faster then. *Maria and the boy were here,* I reasoned as Shad crossed the distance in a gentle lope.

I allowed emotion to let down my guard. That was a mistake.

Still one hundred yards from the cook's cabin the sharp crack of a rifle rang out. I felt the hum of the bullet as it passed close by my head. Shad spooked and crow-hopped ten feet sideways. I nearly lost my seat, but managed to hold on awkwardly as yet another round exploded from behind the clump of brush and boulders to the right of the barn. Tearing my Volcanic rifle from its scabbard, I hurdled from my mount and scrambled to crouch behind a stack of uncut logs. A dog, more wolf than tame by his look, barked fiercely and dashed out from the same cover as the shots. Shad lunged and bolted toward the flume with the dog nipping at his heels as I levered in a .41 caliber reply to the unfriendly messages.

Long moments ticked past in silence until a child's voice called out "Samson! Come here!" The dog left off harrying Shad to return obediently to the brush, and then I heard, "Are you dead, Mister?"

It came to me of a sudden that this was Lucky's boy. "No, sir, I am not."

"I'll remedy that right soon." At that the child let loose with another shot that hit a log just above my head and sent a shower of bark onto my hat.

"Whoa up there!" I cried.

"I got me a clear sight, Mister. You move one inch, and you're a dead man."

I had no intention of moving even an eyebrow until we got this misunderstanding cleared up. My young nephew was a fine shot. His daddy had been, too, at that age.

"Is that you, George?"

"Throw out your piece onto the ground so as I can see it."

I hollered, "You are a fine marksman, George. So was your daddy at your age."

Another bullet answered, gouging a second hole in the bark just a fraction of an inch from the first. The boy shouted, "What would you know about my daddy, you thievin' . . ." Three shots followed in quick succession.

I tossed out my rifle and laid low. *Where was Maria,* I wondered? And just who did the boy imagine me to be?

"George!" I called. "There's my piece. I'm your Uncle John Thornton come at your mother's request." There was a long silence. I tried to communicate once more. "You hear me, boy? I'm your Uncle John."

"Prove it."

How could I prove it? George had never laid eyes on me before, and for the first time I wondered if he had ever even been told of my existence.

"Where is your mother?" I asked.

"Never you mind."

"She'll know me."

There followed a silence, and then, "If you are my uncle, you will know where I come by the name George."

For an instant my mind drew a blank. Who in the Thornton family had been named George? Then the answer came to me in a flash. "You're named after a horse."

His reply was suspicious. "Maybe he told you, or maybe not. There's more to it than that."

Just like Lucky to name his firstborn after a horse, I thought. "Fine animal, King George was. Your daddy won him off a former slaver in a game of chance.

Handsome sorrel . . . Narraganset pacer. Stood sixteen-three hands high. He won the big race in Buffalo. After that we called your daddy Lucky. He vowed he would name his firstborn child George, be it a son or daughter. You would have been Georgia, I reckon, if you'd been a female."

He did not like my speculating and squeezed off another round to focus me.

"What'd you do that for, boy?" I was getting angry now.

"Stick to the facts," he barked.

Wiping the perspiration from my brow I continued. "With the cash we two got enough to buy fare to California on a packet ship. Crossed the Isthmus and came to San Francisco in '49. Left the horse, though. Your daddy was sad to leave that horse behind." I paused at this point. Certainly I had told enough to satisfy him. "Well, boy? Can I come out now?"

After a long consideration, he consented. "Real slow and easy though." He qualified his permission and instructed me to put my hands high up into the air. I was more than a little uneasy as I stepped out into the sunlight. George stayed behind his cover eyeing me.

"As you can see," I said in a syrupy voice, "I am unarmed."

"Take off your hat," he said, "and hold it over your head."

I obeyed. It was clear to me that the cub was badly spooked by something.

A few more moments passed with the wind stirring the aspens. I was about to speak again when I caught sight of movement in the brush. The dog Samson charged out once more to circle me from a dozen feet away, growling with his fangs bared. "Call off your dog, George," I suggested. "Call him off, I say, and come out here."

Then, his gun barrel pointed toward my midsection, my nephew stepped out from behind the boulder. He was smallish and scrawny. His dark brown hair was parted down the center and lacquered with pomade to keep it in place. This was proof positive that his mother was somewhere around. Maria was always one for straight parts and pomade. George's two front permanent teeth had come in, giving him a muley, toothy look when he squinted up at me. And he was dressed like he was going to church—woolen knickers and jacket.

George walked slowly toward me. "Samson," he said finally. "Down, boy." The wolf-critter lay down, but his eyes never left me, and he did not put his teeth away neither.

"I am putting my arms down," I warned. "Keep your dog back."

"Samson, get on the porch." Samson obeyed, but he seemed reluctant to leave off guarding me. I purely did admire that dog, but I will say distance improved my esteem some. "You look like my daddy." George eyed me warily as if he was seeing some image of Lucky returned from the grave.

"Folks have remarked on the resemblance," I said, replacing my hat.

"Except you don't dress like him. And you need a bath."

He was right, but I ignored the jibe. "I admire your choice of weapons. Except a Volcanic repeater is a man's gun. And point that thing somewheres else." He carried a New Haven-made lever-action, identical to mine. Resting with its butt on the ground, that firearm would have been taller than him.

"At least I still got mine. More than you can say." He eyed my discarded rifle.

"You're no bigger than a corn nubbin." As he complied with my demand that he aim the .41 elsewhere, I leaned forward and wrenched the rifle from his hands. He gave a growl and charged me. I picked him up by the seat of his knickers and held him at arm's length.

"Lemme down! You're not my pa!"

"Well, howdo, nephew George! I'm your Uncle John. Not a rabbit nor a squirrel for you to hunt for your supper! Not a bobcat nor a rattlesnake nor any other sort of varmint neither! Uncle John! That's who you was shooting at! I ought to tan your hide!" I gave him a swat on the rump, and the boy squalled.

Samson shot off the porch like a Roman candle aimed straight at my knees. "George," I warned tersely. "Call off your dog or I'll shoot him." I would not really kill such a fine loyal beast . . . I hoped. George kicked and swung at me, but yelled for the dog to go away, which Samson did. "What's the idea drawing a bead on me, boy?"

"I didn't know . . . who you was! Lemme down!" He was a scrapper, this youngster. I appreciated his spunk but held on to him just the same.

"I'll let you go when you take me to your mother."

"She's . . . in the cook shack! I didn't know who you was! She's . . . she's . . . I got to look after her!"

"Hold still or I'll . . ." I did not finish the threat, but images of a willow switch and George's bare behind came to my mind. Scooping up my gun, I carried my nephew toward the shack. Samson growled at me as we passed by.

CHAPTER 3

I should have known there was some good reason for young George to be so protective. If I had thought about it I would have realized that no child raised by Lucky Thornton would so much as point a loaded weapon at another human unless circumstance compelled him to do so.

The instant I walked through the door of that dim little cabin I knew something was powerful wrong. There were dishes piled in the dry sink and a heap of laundry in a wicker washbasket. Pine needles and a few dry leaves had snuck over the threshold and lay scattered on the floor. The small cot where I figured George spent his nights was made up in a childish way, the red woolen blanket all askew.

I heard a soft cooing sound from behind a red and green curtain that concealed an alcove where the cook used to sleep. It came to me that Maria was sick. I knew she would have to be near to dying before she would let so much as one plate sit unwashed. Maria was the daughter of a Texican army officer who had fought beside Sam Houston. She had been raised with a passion for square corners on the mattress, a floor so clean a man could eat supper off it, and a rule that anyone who passed through her door must take off his spurs and muddy boots or else.

"What's wrong with your mama, boy?" I whispered as I placed my nephew on the ground.

"I tried to tell you . . ." His lower lip went out. He cast a sullen look toward the alcove.

"Is she . . ." I took a step forward.

The smallpox epidemic in Kansas territory came to mind; I imagined the marring of that beautiful complexion. Then images of typhus and cholera leapt into my fearful consciousness.

George straightened his shirt and smoothed his lacquered hair, then stepped out smartly to rap on the wall beside the cloth partition. "Mama?" he queried. "You awake, Mama?"

I heard an exhausted sigh and then her voice. It was feeble, but still the song of a lark to my ears. "Hunting, George?" she managed.

"Yes, ma'am." He threw a black look at me.

"Get a squirrel?" How desperately weary she sounded.

"You could say so." George cocked an eyebrow in a superior gesture that reminded me ever so much of Maria at her most haughty. "I have brought back Uncle John Thornton to see you."

Maria gave a little cry. "My dear boy! George, have you brought John?"

I blurted, "That he has, Maria. Caught himself a big squirrel."

"John Thornton? You've come then?"

I doffed my hat and looked guiltily down at my muddy boots. I needed a bath indeed. "Yes, ma'am. I have been a'horseback practically ever since your letter caught up with me."

"Oh! Oh, John!"

I was tempted to throw back the curtain and kneel beside her bed, but I did not stir.

"Shall I fetch a doctor?" I ventured.

Her reply was weak. "No need for that now."

What did she mean? Was she dying? Had I come too late? She began to weep. Soft, womany little sniffles issued from behind the calico curtain.

Wringing my hat in my hands, I took one step toward the recess.

George, as ever the protective wolf cub, thrust out his chest and held up his arms to bar my way. "You can't go in there!" he declared. "You stink, and she ain't done feeding it yet!"

There was the rustle of bedclothes, then Maria whispered, "A moment, John, please."

I was befuddled. "Feeding . . . it?"

"The baby. What do you think?" George spat. "Go wash or you don't get near neither of them."

I called gingerly, "Maria? You got a baby in there?"

She answered me softly. "A baby girl."

George was defensive. "Yesterday night it come. I tried to tell you!" He snatched a bar of lye soap from the bucket and thrust it into my hands. "Now get out and go wash b'fore you come near my baby sister!"

Humbled, I obeyed, backing out of the cabin and walking a wide circle around the snarling Samson. Fact was, I had not had a bath for three months; not since the stray Mexican steer had pulled me out of the saddle into Tobias Creek last summer. And that had not really been a bath since I had kept all my clothes on.

George was right about one thing, I reckon I smelled like a polecat. Fortunately, I had been carrying one clean pair of breeches and a shirt rolled up in my saddle bag which I had meant to wear to Harry Dourty's wedding at Tailholt. I missed the wedding when a heifer delivered her first calf breech and needed my help to pull it out with a loop of rawhide riata around its little hind hoof.

Working around critters, I knew something about birthing. It was never easy. Lord! I thought about Maria in labor alone with no one but a child to give her comfort! I stared with awe through the doorway and called out to George, "Did your mama bring that child into the world all on her own last night, boy?"

Now he replied in a small, tired-sounding voice. "I helped her some. There wasn't much I could do. It was . . . She told me what to do. But . . . there wasn't nobody else if that's what you mean." It was plain from his tone that it had been a long, terrifying night.

With this, his behavior at our first meeting was explained to my satisfaction. Considering the ordeal, it was a pure wonder George had not blown my head clean off. It was no surprise at all that he wanted to protect his mama and baby sister from a dirty, mean-looking stray who had come riding unannounced up the canyon. I thought better of the boy after that.

I carried my clean clothes up the path toward the sheer rock face at the head of the little valley. Standing beneath the broken flume, I scrubbed all over with lye soap and melted snow water, then walked back, shivering and barefoot to the cabin.

As I returned to the cook shack, I thought about my bare shanks and surveyed the ground carefully. I expected an ambush by Samson, but as I drew closer I saw that he was tied to the corral railing.

Rapping gingerly on the doorpost, I was surprised when Maria said in a strong and amused voice, "Who could that be, George?"

"It's John Thornton," I replied, knowing that she was fully aware of who was knocking.

"All washed and curried and presentable, are you?"

"Yes, ma'am. Only I am barefooted, I fear."

"You are forgiven. Come in and welcome," she answered.

I mumbled, "Yes, ma'am." But in a sudden attack of

bashfulness I stared down at my naked toes and hung back long enough that she called to me.

"Are you coming in, John? Or shall I come out?"

I lifted the latch and stepped into the warmth of the room. What I saw surprised me.

In the time I had been washing up, the room had been swept and George stood wiping clean dishes at the sink. The gingham curtain was pulled back to reveal Maria sitting up in bed and holding the little baby in her arms. She looked almost holy to me; like the image of the Madonna and child I had seen once in the mission of the Spanish fathers in Monterey. I felt my heart jump at the sight of her, so beautiful she was. She was weary looking, sure, but she had color in her cheeks, and her luminous dark eyes were filled with the serenity of a woman who had weathered hard times and come out the other side into daylight. Her long black curls cascaded over the shoulders of her white nightgown. The newborn babe of my dead brother rested peacefully in Maria's arms. Its rosebud face was turned toward her breast.

I stood rooted and gawking, shifting nervously from one foot to another.

"Howdo, John." Maria seemed pleased that I had come.

"Are you well?" I stammered.

"George is taking fine care of me." She inclined her head toward my nephew and the dishes and the broom propped in the corner.

There was a long, awkward silence as George

stacked the last plate. "I'll go chop the kindling now, Mother," he said, not acknowledging my presence.

"That will be fine, George." She dismissed him, and he brushed past me without looking at my face.

It took me some time to gather my thoughts and make myself speak. I heard the steady crack of the ax against the wood outside. It came to me that George was a boy any man could be proud of. He was more like Maria than any part of Lucky, I thought.

Maria cleared her throat. "You have come a long way, John. Have you nothing to say now that you are here?"

There was plenty I had wanted to say over the years, but every phrase eluded me. "I went to the ranch looking for you."

"The ranch was sold to pay Lucky's gambling debts."

"I went to Genoa after. Old Twilly said you and the boy were up here at the sawmill. Didn't mention anything about a baby, though."

Her shoulder rose in a barely perceptible shrug. "I had not spoken to anyone in Genoa about my condition. That is not the sort of matter one talks about." There was something momentarily hard in her expression as she said this to me. What was beneath the words?

"You are a courageous woman."

"The Lord helps us bear what we must."

"But why didn't you and the boy stay closer to town . . . to a doctor?"

"After the funeral, Kit was arrested and . . ."

"Kit?" The reference to my baby brother confused me. Last I had seen him he had been younger than George and still with Ma and Pa on the farm back East.

"Didn't I mention Kit in the letter?"

"No."

"Kit had been living with us most of the year when Lucky was murdered. The shock of it made him wild. He is incarcerated in Genoa for making threats and disturbing the peace. The sheriff may have locked him up to keep him from getting killed, but I felt quite unprotected after that."

This news added another dimension to my understanding of why folks were so eager to see me leave Genoa. "How long is he in for?" I pictured Kit as a nine-year-old kid locked up in a sunless cell, but of course he was full growed now.

"Three months was the sentence. He will be out soon."

"I'll see to it." I sensed that there was still more unhappy news for her to tell me. I waited silently while she sorted her words from emotions.

Touching the cheek of the infant, she raised her eyes to meet mine. "After Lucky was . . . after he . . ." She faltered, looked away out the small square window set in the flimsy plank wall. "A woman all dressed in black came to his funeral. She works at Frey's saloon. A dance-hall girl, I heard from Kit. Beautiful, too, though I could not see her face through the veil. Lucky met her at Frey's, you see? Lucky had another woman, and I never knew it until after he was gone. The shame of it was too much to bear. I could not stay in Genoa with George." She cast a furtive glance toward the sound of the wood chopping. "You understand, John. George idolized his father. He must never know of Lucky's faithlessness. This place is the only refuge left to me."

The news of Lucky's philandering ways filled me with such anger that it came to me I would have killed him myself if he was not already dead. Could Maria see the emotion in my face?

"I came soon as I could." My words sounded empty to me.

"I am glad for it." She held out her hand, and for the first time I saw how fragile and wounded she was behind this show of grit. I grasped her fingers. The skin was callused where once it had been soft as silk. I did not let myself gaze on her face, but instead focused on the tiny head of the babe. The sight of such a perfect and innocent being sleeping through such heartache turned my heart to putty. I purely thought I might shed a tear, but I did not. I consoled myself with the thought that you can never trust a man who can look a pretty woman in the eye, so I reckoned I was as reliable as they come.

"She has black hair, like you," I remarked after a time. "A pretty little thing."

Maria smiled. "I have not thought what name to give her. Have you any ideas, John? She should be named after someone good and stronghearted. Is there . . . a good woman you are fond of?"

"I am partial to only one who would be worthy of the honor. Her name is Maria, and I have been faithful only to her all these long years since I parted from her."

She bowed her head as if my clumsy declaration had shamed her. "Please, John . . ." She implored me to be silent.

"Alright, then. I will not open my mouth on the matter again. But . . . what is your full Christian name?"

She became cheerful once more. "Maria Madison Foquette. My father once shook the hand of President James Madison, and the experience never left his mind."

"You were well-named. And this babe could not do better than to be called after her mother." At that, I picked up the baby and held her carefully like she might break. I whispered soft in her little ear. "Madison Thornton we will call you, after a great lady. You will be Maddy for short."

Every good thing I had missed hit me with full force as I laid that baby back in Maria's arms. All those wasted years looking for my fortune had brought me back empty-handed to the place where I had begun. I still had strong feelings for my brother's widow, and this disturbed my peace of mind considerably. The thought lit up my brain that maybe I could just forget the fact that

Lucky had been murdered. Maybe I could just take up where he left off. Guilt immediately slammed into my head like a two-by-four.

"I'll need to be on the road again by morning," I said abruptly. "There are questions to be asked about Lucky. I aim to get to the bottom of it."

"The bottom will still be there in a week or so. Won't you stay awhile, John?" Maria asked in a dreamy voice.

"George might not like it much."

"I could use the help."

"Then I will stay. A week anyway."

She needed sleep and yet would have forced herself to stay awake to keep me company. Under the pretext of needing to hunt up fresh meat for supper, I loaded the old shotgun and left the cabin. Without a word to George I took to the hills to think and pray awhile about what would be best to do. There was an old stump a half mile up the path beyond where the flume jutted out into the void. I sat there as the shadows lengthened, listening to the pop of George's ax echoing from below.

A covey of four dozen quail scurried up on a fallen tree, then down the other side. They paid me no mind. With a single shot I might have brought a dozen home for supper, but I did not raise the muzzle.

Perched on the cedar stub, I set to work considering the dangerous situation in which I found myself. It was not Lucky's murderers I was worried about at the moment, but my own unsteady heart.

It had only been a little more than a week since I got word my brother was killed. Now here I was, come riding in like a knight to the rescue. However, I was not anything like the hero in a Walter Scott story. Instead, after five minutes in Maria's presence, I had found myself thinking how nice it might be to marry Lucky's widow and raise his children! All these things I freely confessed.

The high esteem in which I had held myself sunk to zero.

Maria and her young'uns needed more than a scruffy saddle tramp like me to look after them. It occurred to me that if I settled in with the intention of lending a hand for a week or so I might never want to leave. All those numb places in my soul might wake up permanently. If I spent much time rocking Maddy I would be a goner.

I have found that there are times in life when examining motives and too much soul-searching does not ease a troubled mind. Then a man just has to leave it in the hands of the Lord and do his level best to do what is right no matter how hard it is. As the Book says, there will come the day the Lord will pass all my deeds and motives through the fire and burn up the bad but keep the good.

"Hang it all, John," I said aloud when all the tangle became too much to unravel. "Lucky is lynched. You will find who done it and why, and justice will be served. That is the right thing for you to do."

Having set my priorities straight, I determined that I would sort out the question of comforting the widow and orphans at a later time. Feeling much relieved, I shot two rabbits and brought them to the cook shack.

It was near dark when I got back. Holding the game for Maria to see, I said, "Does fried rabbit sound good to you?"

"I was just dreaming of it."

George, who was reading his McGuffey in the lamplight, commented he would rather have had quail.

I set to work. "These skins will make a warm blanket for your baby sister. Come here, George, and I'll show you how it's done."

"I got to do my lesson," George replied, sullenly pulling the lamp closer to the book.

The boy would be a hard case to win over, I figured. But as I fried up our meal, I could hear Maria humming softly to Maddy, "Bye baby bunting, Daddy's gone a'hunting to find a little bunny skin to wrap my baby bunting in."

CHAPTER 4

I stayed on at the sawmill for nigh onto a week to see after the mother and the child. I believe at first that George resented me as much as if I had been among the men who lynched his father. He did not speak more than two words to me and cast dark looks at me when I conversed with Maria or tended his baby sister. I let him do all the regular chores, chopping wood and keeping the fire burning.

It was clear from the wild geese flying overhead in perfect V formations that winter was coming soon and hard. I repaired the roof and rechinked the logs of the cookhouse. I also inspected the flume on the high bluff, though the view from the edge gave me the fantans. I concluded that the mill could be put in order again, then set that thought aside. It would mean a much longer stay than I was planning. While Maria was still in bed, I also managed the womany stuff, doing laundry and cooking and such as that.

The third day it came to me that I might make friends with my nephew if we were to share some sport. With

Maria's permission I took him hunting, leaving Samson tied up and whining at home. We hiked up the high meadow and then worked our way downslope with the breeze in our faces, as the Indians will do. In this way the deer would not catch our human scent.

Removing a small glass bottle from my ammunition pouch, I anointed George and myself with a few drops of the strong-smelling contents.

George balked. "This stinks worse than you did the first day you rode up."

"A dab of this, and a deer will think you're his grandpa come a'calling." I held up the vial. "Musk. A Cheyenne showed me the trick. Pure ambrosia to a deer. Regular perfume of lilac to a doe. Taken from the scent glands of a killed buck. The glands are little sacks, just under the hide on the belly side of the hind legs and right below the knee. I'll show you how to cut them out when we've got our deer."

After this, George perked up a bit. He studied my bottle of scent and then listened while I showed him the tricks of hunting like an Indian. I showed him how to camouflage himself and explained that a Washoe brave hunted with a bow and arrow and was required to use stealth and brains. This was unlike the white man, who generally blasted away with big guns and killed more than needed.

Two quiet hours passed with us well-hid behind a stand of trees on the slope above the pasture. Along about sundown I spotted a movement of the manzanita brush on the far side. I nudged the boy. First one doe emerged from the shadowed forest and then a second. They lifted their heads to sniff the wind. The breeze had changed, pushing our musky aroma into the clearing. The deer were unconcerned. A fawn scampered out and then another. Three more does followed, and at last, a small forked-horn buck.

George made as if to take aim on the largest doe. I stopped him, indicating that females were not to be taken. This was more than chivalry. There was a reason for this rule in the Indian camps. Female critters were the promise of the future. Bucks, on the other hand, were always too many. It only took one buck to populate an entire herd. The indiscriminate killing of does and fawns by the white immigrants was only one reason the native population had grown to dislike and mistrust the white man.

These were important matters which I would explain to George later. For the moment, however, we turned our attention to the enormous rack of antlers that crowned the head of the largest buck I had ever laid eyes on.

I resisted the temptation to give a whistle of astonishment as the eight-point critter strutted out into the broad grassy space and snorted into the breeze. Like a wise general or a completely immoral bounder, the old stag had sent his harem out first before exposing himself to danger.

I nudged George, indicating that meat for the winter had arrived. The boy raised his weapon, took aim, hesitated, and then looked at me. He spoke in a barely audible whisper. "I can't."

I did not comprehend his meaning right then. My blood was up with the excitement of seeing such a magnificent animal. I drew a bead on the buck; I had a clear shot at its heart too. Then, before I could squeeze off my round, the air erupted with the explosion from George's rifle. In a flash the field was a confusion of white tails waving good-bye, all except for the one deer George had made his target.

The small forked-horn buck reared up then dropped to his knees. One convulsive twitch and he was dead.

"What'd you do that for?" I asked in astonishment. "I had the big one right in my sights."

George lowered his gun and stood up with a sigh. "He's lived a long time," he said. "We didn't need so much meat. Leave it at that."

My appreciation of George deepened after that. He was right, of course. I consoled myself that the old buck would have been tough to chew on anyway, but I have never again had such an animal in my sights.

We hung the forked-horn from a tree, bled him, and cleaned him. I showed George how to take the scent glands, then we hoisted the carcass on up to the top of the tree and left it there overnight to chill when the temperature dropped to thirty-eight degrees. We camped all night up on the mountain. Next day we returned with Shad to tote the deer back to the sawmill.

In the butchering room in the barn I taught George

the proper way to skin and quarter the autumn-cooled meat. It surprised him that butchering a deer was not much more complicated than cutting up a chicken for frying—only bigger. Soon enough George was hard at work sawing the front quarters into blade roasts, arm roasts, and steaks. He sectioned up the ribs for spare ribs and stew meat, which we canned. There was quite a collection of soup bones in the bone box, besides the ones I used to finally win over Samson. I was satisfied that George could repeat the process on his own if he had to. This was a relief to me. Not one particle of the deer was wasted, and when it came time for me to leave, he would be more capable of caring for his mother should I not return.

George admired the antler handle of my skinning knife. "Would you make me one like yours?" he asked.

I promised him I would do so and sawed off the largest piece of tine.

Showing George how to preserve the hide, we scraped it clean and rubbed it with pickling salt. I explained he must tan and keep the buckskin as a remembrance, because this was his first buck and he hunted in a manly and respectful way. I was proud of him and said as much. It came to me that Lucky would have been proud too. My approval pleased George, I think, and we became friends.

That night I fried up fresh liver and onions. As we ate I sat quietly while he told his mother all about the musk scent and the Indian way of hunting and the old buck who we named Old Man of the Mountain.

As young George rattled on in the soft firelight I thought I saw Maria study me in a kindly, almost loving, manner. When I turned to look at her, she glanced away, and the spell was broken. Perhaps it was only my hopeful imagination.

As I held little Maddy in my arms I realized that I had not felt such warmth in many lonely years. That night as Maria prayed at the bedside of George, she thanked God for answering her prayer and sending me to them. The last thing I would ever call myself was an answer to a prayer. *Could she mean it,* I wondered? Trying to put thoughts of her from my mind, I headed out to bunk in the stall next to Shad.

Over the next several days George and I jerked the toughest cuts of venison, smoking it slow over a mesquite fire. I did not forget to toss some scraps to Samson along the way.

When Maria was well enough, I saddled up to head back to Genoa to take up the trail of my brother's murderers. I do believe Maria and George were sorry to see me go.

If I had known what danger awaited Maria, George, and little Maddy, I would never have ridden out that morning. I had no reason to suspect any harm would come to them, however, and the last word I said to George was this: "I'll be coming back soon enough with Kit in tow, I reckon. This time I expect that you will keep your rifle hanging on the pegs instead of trying to blow our heads off."

My admonition must have come back to the boy the first time he laid eyes on the two riders who approached from the ridge above the sawmill. George, who was gathering dry bark for kindling, did not pay the strangers any mind as their mounts carried them down the steep slope of the upper trail. My nephew left the rifle on the wall just like I had told him to do.

I was a full hour's travel toward Genoa when Rough Elliott and a slimy Mississippi gambler by the name of Bernard King stopped to water their horses in the trough beside the barn. George eyed them from the woodpile and thought about the rifle, but the memory of my words kept him from doing what instinct told him he ought to do to protect his mother and baby sister.

Samson was tied up near the front door, but his alarmed barking penetrated the walls of the cook shack. Maria, her hands covered in flour from the kneading trough, stepped outside to join her boy.

"Who is it, George?" she asked him. The afternoon sun was bright behind the intruders, making it hard to see their faces.

Had she identified King, she would have gone inside and thrown the bolt across the door. But it was too late by the time she recognized the man standing near the corral. King was the same fellow Lucky had once called "the most crooked, no-good, thimble-rigging, card-sharp anywhere west of the Mississippi."

Bernard King was a cheat and a bully. He was skilled at his deception and because of this was a wealthy man. Lucky discovered it too late to save his fortunes. He had lost his ranch to King in a game of five-card draw in the back room of Frey's some six months before. Even the ranch had not paid all that Lucky owed to King, however. Lucky was murdered while still in debt to the little weasel.

Today, King had come to pay a call on Lucky Thornton's widow in order to collect the balance of what was due him. Maria had a reputation as a woman not to be trifled with. For that reason, cowardly as he was, King had brought Rough Elliott along to back him up in his claims.

Maria tried to withdraw when she saw who the callers were. "George," she said quietly, "come inside."

George had no knowledge of all the misery his father had brought upon the family. The boy did not know the coarse characters with whom Lucky had consorted. Worst of all, the boy did not move fast enough to avoid the grasp of Elliott.

As George turned to obey his mother, Elliott lit out after him, grabbing him up by the scruff of his neck and holding him up at eye level.

"Well, look what I done cotched myself, King. A lee-tle pup."

Samson snarled and his barking took on a frenzied tone. He flung himself at the leash time after time, attempting to break free of the restraint.

If Maria had fired a cannon, I would not have heard her. She knew too well that I would not be back until a full day and night had passed. A woman alone, still weak from childbirth, there was no one to whom Maria could turn for protection but the Lord. As she watched her boy struggle against Rough Elliott she resolved that she would trust God and do her level best to defend herself and her children against those who threatened them. Instantly the words of the psalmist leapt to her mind, "He has taught my hands to war and my fingers to fight so that a bow of steel is broken in my hands."

In that same moment she knew she was not alone. Someone unseen, and yet mighty, stood beside her on the porch. She felt the presence and was no longer afraid. Courage filled her, and Maria hollered out in a voice so fierce that it startled the attackers, "Put him down, sir!"

King spit in the watering trough to show he did not pay Maria's protest any mind. He delicately stroked his waxed mustache with the back of his hand and swaggered over to where Elliott held my nephew. Laughing, King patted the struggling boy on the cheek and remarked, "This pup is like to need drowning, Rough. What you think? Should we cull the thing or just keep him for ransom till his mama pays what I am owed?"

Jerking his chin downward sharply, King gave the signal for Elliott to plunge George into the trough. The boy came up sputtering and coughing, but no less feisty than before. The two men laughed at the boy's ineffectual kicks and punches. Then Elliott stopped laughing suddenly when one of George's little pointy-toed boots connected with the same spot on Elliott's chin as the nail keg had arrived. Elliott angrily dashed my nephew into the tub again.

At that moment Samson surged against the rope that held him, and this time the cord parted. He took off at full speed, like a runaway buzzsaw, straight toward Rough Elliott.

Bernard King backed away from the sudden onslaught, but a flick of his wrist, and a hideout gun appeared in his palm. As Samson charged, King fired the derringer. His first shot hit the dog in the side and spun him around. The second bullet killed him.

George called out, "Samson! Samson!" and he began to wail and kick furiously.

Maria did not speak another word. She turned on her heel and went in to fetch the lever action. Snatching it from the wall, she emerged with it at the ready. "Put him down!" she demanded as Elliott was again about to treat George like a load of Saturday wash. Her voice was strong and sure.

Both men glanced up from their sport and their grins melted. "Well now, Missus . . ." King spread his hands out in a way to show that he was only joking. "We can talk this over quietly."

"Put down my son."

George continued to struggle through this. He managed to sink his teeth into Elliott's black and filthy thumb. Elliott gave a yelp and booted the boy hard on the behind. George's fight was to no avail. Elliott gave him a shake and cursed him.

King replied, "Where is your hospitality, Missus Thornton? I figgered we might discuss our problem over a meal. Do I smell venison stew?"

"I am serving forty-one caliber Volcanic repeater pudding, if you have an appetite for it, Mister King. I am a crack shot."

King let out a nervous laugh, as if he did not believe her. "Come now, Missus Thornton. We know your brother-in-law is no longer here to take your part in this quarrel."

At that, Maria gave him fair warning. "First shot will be three inches to the right of your boot, Mister King." The cartridge exploded, the bullet tearing the ground right where she predicted.

King jumped back, his tall stovepipe hat falling to the ground. Maria drilled the top hat with a second shot, sending the thing rolling toward the rail fence of the corral.

"Next shot will be clean through your kneecap, Mister King."

"That hat came from Saint Louis!" he cried.

"You'll be showing it off for Saint Peter if you press me further, Mister King."

King was white with a combination of humiliation

and rage. "I don't take kindly to a woman who tries to best me," the gambler declared.

"Then you should not trifle with a woman who is your better."

"I heard you were a religious person," King scolded, pretending shock and outrage. "Never heard of a true Christian woman to shoot a man."

She pivoted to direct her aim at Rough Elliott's shinbone. "Mister Elliott," she said. "What Mister King says is true; I do not hold with killing. But I can blow your leg off without feeling a twinge if you threaten my boy with harm anymore."

Elliott blurted, "She means it."

"Right," Maria confirmed. "And my second shot will be you, Mister King. At least there will still be two good legs left between you."

George dangled from the end of Elliott's meaty paw.

King said, "I can see you are not going to be sensible nor reasonable."

Maria was smiling from behind the sights. "That is correct. You have shot my dog, and now I am inclined to make a gelding out of you unless you do exactly as I command. Now . . . let go of George. Then reach high in the air."

Rough Elliott lowered George gently to the ground, then both men stood with their hands up, waiting for instruction.

Maria continued in a sweet, motherly voice. "George, step away from the gentlemen, if you please."

"Yes, ma'am." The boy obeyed, giving his mother a clear field of fire.

Elliott muttered to King. "You ain't gonna tell no one about what she done, are you, King?"

King's eyes narrowed as he threatened her. "We'll be back. I got the law on my side."

Maria replied, "I know your sort of law. The same law that lynched my husband!" She fairly spat out the words. "Back up," she ordered. "Get on your horses and ride out of here! And know this! From the time you saddle up until you are out of my sight there's a forty-one caliber aimed at your backsides. Turn around, and I'll serve you up a dish you will not soon forget!"

The duo obeyed her, riding without looking back until they were certain they were out of range. For the moment, she and the young'uns were safe.

CHAPTER 5

When I had last seen Kit he was only nine years old. Mostly my mind still saw him as a boy in knee britches. But when I gave him serious consideration, I imagined him going to some Eastern school, becoming a teacher or a lawyer perhaps.

His given name was Christopher, and he was named partly in honor of the famous scout, Kit Carson. Carson's given name was also Christopher, and our Kit had been born small, just like the illustrious mountain man. My brother Lucky and I had held out for calling him Runt, but Mama seemed not to care for that idea.

And now here he was, not only out West, but in Genoa and in jail. I did not know if Lucky had enticed him to come to the territory with tales of strike-it-rich, or if he had come of age with the same wanderlust that afflicted his elder kin, but he was in deep now and no mistake.

Maria had told me that Kit was being held for threatening folks with a pistol and for being drunk and disorderly. None of those were hanging offenses, it seemed to me, but given the state of things in the Carson Valley, I was not too sure.

I was thankful that Si Denton was still town constable. He was a good man and a fair one, and I could not believe that he was involved in Lucky's death. The manner of it was not Si's style. He would have held Lucky for the Territorial Marshal even if he had been convinced of Lucky's guilt.

The Carson County courthouse was a two-story brick structure at the east end of town. The front was all offices and courtroom and such. At the back, on the ground floor, was the jail. Shad and I circled to the rear of the building and approached the steel door that was the only outside entrance to the prison.

I hammered on the metal with my fist, and a small spy panel opened. I thought I recognized Si's pale blue eyes, but he seemed unable to place me. "What d'ya want?"

"Don't you know me, Si?" I asked. "John Thornton. I hear tell my brother is a guest of yours."

Si gave the same wheezy chuckle that had always passed for his laugh, then I heard the sound of bolts being thrown back, and the door opened. "Well, John," he said. "After three months had gone by, I had hopes that you weren't coming."

"Why say it like that, Si?"

He shook his thinning crop of gray strands, and his dark-complected face looked sorrowful to me. "No good will come of it," he said. "Let the dead bury the dead.

Take your brother, and Maria, too, if she'll go, and get out of here. We don't want trouble in this town."

"Si," I protested, "I'm not looking for trouble, but I do want some answers. Now if you don't mind, I'd like to see my brother and then talk to you some more."

"Fine," he agreed, leading me to the rear of the dark room and pointing me toward where a steel wall rose from floor to ceiling. The Genoa jail consisted of two side-by-side metal cubes. Each cell was no more than six feet wide and eight deep. The one up against the outside wall was empty; the other held my brother.

I peered in through the barred window in the otherwise solid door. Inside, sitting on the cot that was the only piece of furniture, I saw a thin young man with his head in his hands. He was pale compared to me and Lucky and slighter of build. If I had got the height and Lucky the bulk, Kit seemed to have neither.

"Kit," I called to him.

"Go away," he said without looking up. "I'm not hungry, and I don't feel like talking."

"Kit," I said again. "I'm your brother."

He looked up sharp at that. "My . . . ?"

"I'm John," I explained. "I came when I got Maria's letter. I saw her already, and she told me about you."

He stood up and regarded me through the bars. "Is she alright? I mean the baby and all?"

"She's fine," I assured him. It pleased me in some deep down way that even locked up as he was, Kit had asked after Maria's welfare.

"Can you get me out of here?" he continued.

I turned to look at Si, who pursed his lips and frowned. "Sentence is almost up. I suppose I could release him into your custody," he said doubtfully. "But I think he's safer here."

"Safer!" Kit shouted, flinging himself up against the door of the cell. "Safer for the murderers who killed Lucky. You're protecting them! Letting them cover their tracks. Let me out so I can get after them again!"

Si said, "You see what a temper he's got? He was waving a six-shooter around on Main Street, yelling that he was gonna make somebody talk. Then he threatened the Major and some others. I don't know how much of it he meant . . ."

"Just give me a gun, and I'll show you how much!" Kit interrupted angrily. "I'll show all those butchers when I catch up with them."

Si raised his eyebrows as much as to say, "See what I mean?"

I shrugged and turned away from the door. "You're right, Si," I agreed. "He's safer in here. Leave him be for now."

"Hey! What kind of brother are you? Are you on their side?"

"Simmer down," I suggested. "I'll be back later. Come on, Si. I'd still like to talk to you."

We went into the front half of the courthouse then into Si's office. We had to close two doors on the way, just to shut out the noise of Kit's cussing us.

After we had shut the door behind us, Si sank into the oak rolling chair behind his desk and waved me toward a bench. "What happened here, Si?" I questioned. "Maria could only tell me what the result was, not the why of it . . . or the who."

Si steepled his fingers together and frowned. "You know your brother was a gambler," he began. "And sometimes he ran with a pretty seedy bunch like Lute Olds and Sam McWade."

"Yes, and he also owned two houses, a sawmill, and a ranch," I retorted. "He was friends with Judge Hyde, Elwood Knott, and Justice Van Sickle. I even seem to recall that he elk hunted with a certain town constable, Si!" Si turned his head to look up at a rack of elk antlers that stretched from halfway up the wall clear to the eight-foot-high ceiling. "You telling me Lucky was hanged for who he played cards with?"

"No, no!" Si protested. "Look, I'll tell you what I heard, not what I know for fact, all right?"

"Fair enough."

"Your brother was accused of being involved in the murder of a rancher named Gordier up in Hope Valley . . . of having plotted the man's death so as to steal his cattle herd."

"Was there any proof?"

Si thumped his meaty palm flat down on the desk top. "Of course not! If there had been anything more to it than gossip, I would have seen to it personal. The fact is, the rancher was killed, and your brother had been to see him a week before he was bushwhacked."

"What's that prove?"

"Not a thing. Then Lucky brought me this." Si pulled open the center desk drawer and drew out a paper. He hesitated over showing it to me, then finally turned it around so I could see. It read: *Lucky Thornton, you are a thief and a murderer, but justice will overtake you in the end if you don't clear out at once.* It was signed, *The Committee.*

"What'd you do?"

Si made a face like he had bit into a sour apple. "Lucky showed it to me, but he was laughing about it. Said he didn't scare easy and for certain not by midnight callers who hid their real names behind fancy titles. I told him he ought to go away for a time till things settled down some, but he never heeded me."

"Maria never saw this."

"No. Lucky said he didn't want to frighten her or the boy. Asked me not to say anything about it where she would hear it either. 'Course that tied my hands pretty fair."

I thought about what Si had said. It was just like my headstrong and proud brother to want to face up to things without any help. "Did he try to find out who had sent it?"

"If he did, he didn't tell me."

Now here was the main matter. I stared at my boot

toes for a minute before I quietly asked, "And what have you done about his lynching?"

I studied Si's face like I know how to judge. His eyes showed real pain. "I can't find out anything. Nobody saw anything, or if they did, they are scared to talk about it. I wasn't even in the county the night . . ."

"Why not?"

Si worked his jaw like he was chewing his words instead of a plug of tobacco. "I got a line on a border ruffian name of Edwards. The word was that he was up in the Honey Lake country, so me and Paul and Knott and some others rode up there, but it was a cold trail."

"Who's this Edwards?"

"He's a wanted man from a killing over in Placerville." There was a long pause before Si continued. "And he's the one said to have dropped the hammer on Gordier."

"That's mighty convenient, don't you think?" I exploded. "You and Lucky's friends sent off on a wild-goose chase the same night this committee lynches Lucky!" Then another thought struck me, "Who told you about Edwards?"

Si shook his head. "If you think you can connect that information to the nightriders, you're mistaken. It came by Snowshoe Thompson."

Just then the door to Si's office burst open, and in rushed a lean, young man, aged twenty-five or so, with a pair of pistols on his hips and a flush on his face. "Si!" he shouted, right up against Si's desk and in front of me,

"John Thornton's in town, looking for trouble. A week ago he busted up Twilly's store and scared Missus Frey half to death. We've got to bring him in pronto!"

I smiled and looked to see what Si was going to say now. He was grinning too. "Did you bust up Twilly's?" he asked me.

"Not by a jugful! Some character name of Rough Elliott was leaning on Twilly to find out about me. I just cooled him out some."

"You!" the young fella said stabbing at me with his index finger. "You're Thornton!" He went to slap leather, but I saw it coming. By leaning forward in my chair I grabbed both his wrists and held his hands down at his sides.

"Who is this temperamental character?" I asked as the blond-haired man struggled to draw his pistols and got even more flushed in the process.

"Paul!" Si snapped. "Settle down and leave your Colts holstered, or you're through working for me!" Then to me he said, "John, meet my deputy, Paul Hawkins . . . who if he is going to remain my deputy," he added pointedly, "had better not be so quick to be on the shoot!"

As I felt Hawkins' muscles relax, I let go my grip and turned him loose. "But he's a killer, same as his brother!" he argued.

Si looked disgusted. In a heavy, no-nonsense tone he ordered, "Wait outside, Paul. Better yet, go on over to the hotel and get my supper."

"But . . . !"

"Git!" Si concluded.

Hawkins went, but with bad grace, slamming the door behind him. "Seems he must think my brother got what he deserved," I remarked.

"Don't be too rough on Paul," Si cautioned. "He's hot-headed, but he's a straight arrow when it comes to the law, and he was with me the night of the hanging."

I still had my doubts about Hawkins, but I kept silent. "And what about this Elliott?"

"He's a bad 'un. Drifted into town six months back. Caught a job with the Major. I hear he's foreman now. Watch out for him. He came with a bad reputation."

"Like me, Si?" I asked with a grin. "I guess that's all for now. If you'll let me, I'll take responsibility for Kit."

"He's likely to be a handful. You sure you can manage him?"

I nodded.

"I'll have to keep his pistol," Si paused. "And yours, if you're packing." Then a look of remembrance passed over his face. "You still handy with a rifle?" he asked slowly.

Shrugging I agreed. "Need to be, up in the high lonely," I said.

Si set his jaw. "Then I want you to fetch in your piece for as long as you're staying in town."

"That isn't friendly, Si," I complained, but he did not rise to the humor. "It's outside with Shad. You take good care of it."

"There's one more thing," Si said. "Don't spread this around, but we've got Indian trouble. Six times in the past few months tenderfeet coming over the trail have had their stock run off in the night. The seventh was last week, and three men got wounded."

"Why tell me this?"

Si shook his head. "There's present trouble enough in the world," he said. "Let the past alone. Let the dead stay dead."

I stood and said stiffly, "I need to get back to Maria."

At the mention of Maria's name, Si's face clouded again, and he stared down at the torn and faded blotter on his desk top. "John," he said quietly as I turned to leave. "You won't tell Maria that I knew before the hanging . . . about the warning, I mean?"

"No, Si," I agreed. "She doesn't need to know."

CHAPTER 6

Kit groused more than a little about not getting his weapon back. "Whose gun?" I said, teasing him. "Si remarked that when you were waving it around, it looked a mite . . . heavy for you."

My little brother seemed a touch embarrassed, but just as hostile as ever. "So it was Lucky's . . . but it's mine now! And I aim to use it to catch the dirty snakes who killed him."

"Easy," I said, shushing him as Si closed the steel door of the jail behind us. "Don't give the constable a reason to throw you back in the hoosegow. Come with me over to the hotel. You could use a decent meal, couldn't you?"

Though disposed to stay on the prod, Kit's stomach betrayed him by growling. "All right," he grudgingly agreed. "And . . . thanks for getting me out." Then he froze in his tracks as if he'd just spotted a sidewinder at his feet. "To the hotel . . . you mean Frey's place?"

"You think he was involved in Lucky's murder, right?

Well, if you're gonna beard the lion," I said, "you gotta do it in his den."

The clink of my spurs sang a soft tune to the evening as we walked to the hotel with me leading Shad. The horse's head bobbed in time to the music.

"You know that's where the gal . . ." His words trailed off. Perhaps he thought he was speaking ill of the dead to mention Lucky's infidelity.

"I heard about Nell," I pointed out. "Maria has had a load to carry, but she is tougher than you think too. Now I have the same intentions as you," I said. "To see justice done and Lucky's killers brought in. But we need to go about it smart. You get further by listening than by shooting off your mouth. Savvy?"

On the way down Main Street we passed Terwilliger's. The shutters were closed over the windows, and the front entry was double-locked and barred. "Looks like Twilly figgers on an early winter," I observed.

"How do you mean?"

I thumbed the sign tacked to a doorpost which read GONE AWAY ON BIZZNESS. "The bird has flown south till the storm blows over."

The Frey hotel was a two-story affair with saloon and dining room on the ground floor. Upstairs there were a dozen rooms for travelers' lodgings and Major Frey's office. A hall separated the saloon to the left from the eatery to the right. As we entered I spared a glance for occupants of the bar. There was the usual assortment of hangers-on: two cowhands leaning over the counter like they were in dire need of its support, two hurdy-gurdy gals bent on relieving those cowpokes of their pay, a barkeep with elegant curled mustaches, and a table of poker players in the far corner. I wanted to see if anyone took note of us. None did, except one of the card players. He was a weaselly looking feller with waxed mustache and Imperial that matched his slicked down hair. He looked up at me, then ducked his head sharp as if afraid I might recognize him, but I did not.

I pushed into the saloon and said loudly to the barkeep, "My name's John Thornton. Is the Major about?"

"Gone home for the evening," the bar man said in a friendly tone. My name seemed not to mean anything to him, but the slick-looking gambler stiffened in his chair, and so did one of the saloon gals.

"That's her!" Kit hissed in my ear. Then louder he complained, "Are we drinkin' or eatin'? What are you lookin' at anyhow? Come on, John. I'm hungry."

I turned and gave him a good-natured shove across the hall into the restaurant. "For a man who might still be eating cold beans and drinking spring water inside a steel cage, you're awful free with your complaints."

Just behind me in the bar I heard the slick fella say, "Cash me in."

Someone else retorted, "Where do you get off quitting now, King? Sit down and play cards."

The dining room was empty except for us. Kit pulled a chair out from a table in the middle of the room. I shook my head and moved him over to a corner out of view from the corridor. Nobody could get behind me there, and I could watch all the windows. I could also get the first look at whoever came in, before they spotted me.

The floor squeaked under our chairs when we sat down, and a pretty red-haired gal poked her head in from the kitchen. "Be right with you, gents," she said.

"So what can you tell me about Lucky's business dealings?" I asked Kit.

He shook his head and frowned with frustration. "Not enough, I reckon. I hadn't been out here that long. I know the mill had gone bust, and Lucky lost the ranch gambling."

"Why? Why put up the ranch?"

"Said he needed the money for something really big, a cattle deal. He told Maria and me not to worry, that he'd be back on top again soon. 'Course he was still saying that right up until . . . you know."

The red-haired gal, youngish and cute, came over to our table. I judged her to be about Kit's age, or maybe a year younger. My brother, I noticed, was right taken with her smile. "What'll you have?" she wanted to know.

"Beefsteak for me," I allowed. "And potatoes if you got 'em."

"We do," she agreed, "and pumpkin pie for dessert."

"You're reading my mind," I said.

"How about you?" she asked Kit.

"Perfect," he mumbled like a moonstruck calf, staring up at her green-and-gold-flecked eyes.

I kicked his shin under the table. "The lady didn't ask what you thought of the weather, she wants to take your order."

Kit jumped like I remembered he always did when caught with his hand in the cookie jar. "Uh," he stammered.

"Shoot, he'll have the same as me," I said. "And miss, if it isn't too forward, would you mind telling me your name? My brother here won't be able to carry on any kind of conversation until he knows."

She laughed. "I'm Angela Frey," she said. "Angie to my friends. My uncle is Major Frey. And you are?"

"John Thornton," I said without blinking. "The mute here is my brother Christopher . . . Kit."

"Pleased to meet you both," she concluded before bustling off to the kitchen.

I turned to reproach Kit for being so tongue-tied, only to find him wiping his face with both hands. "What ails you?" I demanded.

"She's the most beautiful girl I've ever seen," he moaned.

"Is that cause for lament?"

"Don't you see? She's the Major's niece . . . and he is the one behind the killing of Lucky!"

I reflected on the fact that young Lawrence Frey had gone straight to the Major with news of my visit to the ranch and that Rough Elliott was sure enough nerved up about my presence in town. Still, none of this was proof. "Slow down," I cautioned. "You don't know for certain. Anyway, she doesn't recognize the Thornton name, so don't get crushed so easy. What do you know about this man Gordier and the cattle?"

Kit studied the oil lamps hanging from the wagon-wheel chandelier. "Lucky planned to get his business going again by selling cattle to the emigrants coming through. Gordier had a herd up in Hope Valley that Lucky understood was for sale."

"Why?" I wanted to know. "Why would Gordier not sell the cow critters to the emigrants himself?"

Kit shrugged. "Lucky heard the man was in a big hurry to get back East and needed the cash, but when we rode up there we couldn't agree on a price."

"And after?"

"We came straight back here, and then, a week later, we heard that Gordier had been killed."

"And what do you know about Edwards?"

Kit frowned and said he was not sure. He knew that Edwards was the man accused of murdering Gordier, but he was not certain whether Lucky had ever mentioned Edwards before the shooting.

Nell, the dance-hall gal, entered the dining room. She looked both ways, as if to make certain there was nobody hiding under the tables, then came straight to my side. "You know who I am?" she asked.

"I do," I agreed.

"Then believe me when I tell you that your life is in danger if you stay here in Genoa."

"You don't say," I said with a smile. "Why don't you sit and explain why that should be." I stood and offered her a chair, but she backed away sudden with an angry look.

"It's not funny. Nobody put me up to this to try and scare you. Talking to you could get me fired . . . or worse, only I'm leaving town tomorrow myself, on the early stage."

I tried to match the earnest quality of her message. "We could really use your help," I said. "Finding out who killed our brother."

"Don't be stupid," she said. "Get out of the territory, and take anyone else named Thornton with you."

Another man came into the dining room about then. It was King, the little, oily-looking gambler I had seen in the saloon.

Nell caught one glimpse of his entrance and she swirled away toward the kitchen as if she had passed our table without stopping.

King sat down across the room from us. Every time I looked up I caught him looking at me. The dapper-dressed fella seemed pretty harmless right then, so I chose to ignore him and said nothing to Kit either.

I resumed my conversation with my brother. "Anybody ever catch Edwards, or know if he really even exists?"

Kit shook his head, but I'm not sure if he even heard the question, because Angie came across the plank floor with a big camp kettle of coffee and a pair of mugs. "You two care to have coffee?"

"Please," Kit said, jumping up. "Let me tote that for you. It looks real heavy."

"Oh, no," Angie protested. "You don't need to do that."

But Kit had already popped to his feet and swept the handle of the enameled pot out of her grip. He poured me a cup and one for himself, then gestured for her to lead the way back to the kitchen.

Now, even while listening to my lovestruck brother, I had been keeping an eye on the other table. I watched King hitch his chair around a bit. Kit's path back of Angie took him right beside where the gambler was sitting. I toyed with my coffee cup and watched.

Just after the girl passed by, the toe of the gambler's boot snaked out and hooked Kit's ankle. My brother shouted and pitched forward. Being young and limber, he swung around real sharp and managed to set that coffee pot down without sluicing it all over the floor, even if he did sprawl down there himself. No more than a few drops splashed on the cardsharp, but he reared back like he'd been scalded. "You clumsy oaf!" he yelled. "Why don't you watch what you're doing?"

"You tripped me on purpose," Kit retorted, jumping up all pepper and vinegar.

The gambler did not respond by leaping to his feet at the challenge. Instead he leaned back in his chair and hooked his thumbs in his waistcoat just at chest height.

"You're that same Thornton kid who was waving a gun around town," the card player said. "You're as crazy as your brother was crooked."

Kit started forward with his fists clinched, but I saw the outward flick of the gambler's wrist. It's a good thing I have always had a fair throwing arm, because I whipped my coffee mug around and hit the card player in the forehead just as he was sliding the hide-out gun out of his sleeve. His arm flew up toward his face and the little two-barreled pistol arced in the air and clattered across two table tops. Angie snatched it up.

Kit jumped in the middle of the man then, knocking him over backwards in the chair and falling on top of him. I could not be sure that the gambler did not have another gun somewhere or a knife in his boot, but I had evened things up for the moment.

My brother and the card player were much of the same build, but Kit's blood was up and his fists were flying around the man's ears and nose. King clutched Kit around the neck and the two of them rolled over, scattering chairs.

There was the rush of boot steps from the saloon and a half dozen faces poked into the restaurant to watch the fun. I shoved a table across the floor to block the doorway and keep the fight from escalating into a brawl. "Private affair," I said, folding my arms across my chest.

Kit came up on top again, looking even angrier than before. "You low-down snake," he said. "I oughta tear your head off." He looked like he might do it too. How he could talk and fight at the same time, I'll never know. It made me think that maybe he was tougher than he appeared after all.

"Hold it, Kit," I warned. "Before you strangle him, let's find out who this skunk is and why he went to pick a fight with you."

"His name is Bernard King," Angie spoke up.

King looked at her as if she was a traitor.

"Miss Angie," he retorted. "Your uncle won't like you taking up for any of the Thorntons."

Keeping a wary eye on King, Kit got to his feet. King may have gotten in a lucky punch, because Kit's nose was bloodied some, but then he might have done it when he first hit the floor.

Si Denton's voice bellowed in the hallway. "Break it up! Get out of my way! Let me by here!"

"Howdy, Si," I welcomed him, moving the table aside.

"John!" he said with amazement. "Can't you keep this young hoodlum out of trouble for even one hour?"

"Just hold on there, Si," I advised. "The other fella started it."

"That's a lie!" King interrupted.

"And," I continued, "he drew a gun besides." I gestured toward the pistol that Angie was still holding.

"Self-defense!" the gambler claimed.

"Have you eaten yet?" Si asked me, making his read of the situation.

"Nope," I allowed.

"Neither have I," King protested.

"He hasn't even ordered yet, Mister Denton," Angie pointed out. King gave her a withering look.

"King, you go eat somewheres else," Si concluded. "And John, I told you I don't want any trouble in my town."

"No trouble, Si," I agreed. "We're just in town to have a meal and do some business, that's all."

"Keep it that way."

Kit thought we'd be leaving for the sawmill right after dinner, but two things kept us in town. First was, it was a lonely road and worse at night. Why make things easy for a bushwhacker intent on mischief? Second, it came to me that Miss Nell had laid uncommon stress on the word *early* when she announced her travel plans. I intended to see if I might catch a word with her before she left.

I let it be known that we were staying the night in the livery stable, but of course we did not. Kit and I slept out under the stars at the clear opposite end of town.

CHAPTER 7

The stage was late, and I found Miss Nell sitting atop her trunk some distance apart from the more respectable passengers. I caught her eye upon me as I emerged from the livery stable across the street. Remembering how skittish she had been about speaking to me in public, I strode first to the ticket window where I asked what the fare to Sacramento might be. The clerk named a price, and I told him I would be back when my plans were firmed up. Was it my imagination, or did he seem relieved that I might be leaving town soon? He smiled and told me there would be a place reserved for me on the outbound stage anytime I wished to go.

Thanking him, I turned and caught a glimpse of Miss Nell's kelly-green, satin hoopskirt as she scooted down the alleyway between the freight office and the meat market of Lute Olds. She cast a backwards glance my way. This informed me that Miss Nell would be waiting to have a word with me out back.

I did not follow her directly, but entered the meat market and engaged in conversation with Lute about the going price of beef on the hoof in California. The cattle business was of interest to me, I explained. My statement sent a flash of some unexplained alarm across the features of the butcher.

Without preamble he said, "If Lucky was here, he would want me to tell you that you're makin' some people nervous by poking your nose where it don't belong."

"I hear you were a friend of my brother's."

"As much a friend as Lucky ever had." His face screwed up with some terrible thought. He swallowed hard and said, "I got a beef to cut. So long."

I thanked Lute Olds for his indulgence and then left his establishment the back way.

Miss Nell was waiting for me. She stood by the rear entrance of the freight company. I walked towards her as though I meant to go past. Tipping my hat, I greeted her politely.

She gave her head a slight shake. "Lord a'mighty," she said in an amused voice. "You do look like Lucky."

"Enough so as some gentlemen here abouts get nervous when they lay eyes on me."

"I don't wonder." That painted mouth of hers turned up in a wide grin. "Order a side of beef from Lute, did you?"

"Small talk is all. Wanted to come out this way so as not to draw attention."

She laughed. "I'll bet Lute is all in a sweat."

"He's in on it?"

"It?" She was playing coy.

"Whatever it was that got Lucky killed."

"I'll tell you what got him killed." She tossed her head and gazed thoughtfully towards the weather vane atop the livery barn. "He wanted to know which way the wind blew. He asked too many questions."

"Never hurts to ask."

She shrugged. "Curiosity killed the cat."

"Some cats have nine lives, I hear."

"Lucky used his all up. And you can take this little word of advice along with you: Do what I'm doing. Leave the territory before you use up your lives too."

"I want answers."

"Then ask Lucky. You'll be meeting up with him soon enough."

"Why was he hanged?" I grasped her arm and held tight.

"Let go my arm . . ."

I said, "Lucky was no murderer."

"I told you. He knew too much."

"That's no crime."

"Depends on what you know about whom and what you intend to do with the information."

"Blackmail? You're saying Lucky was a blackmailer?"

"And, thanks to me, someone was blackmailing Lucky right back. The problem is, I came to be fond of your brother. Furthermore, I came to pity that wife of his."

"Then help me. What did Lucky know?"

"Those details I was not privy to, else I might be strumming a harp on some cloud, myself. I don't want to know more than I know."

Sensing she was telling the truth, I stepped away from her. She smoothed the satin of her sleeve where my hand had been, then she straightened her hat. "I was paid a'plenty to lure your brother away. It was not a difficult task, which leads me to believe he was no stranger to living a secret life."

"Who paid you?"

"Come now, Mister Thornton. You're not altogether a fool."

I was certain she was speaking of Major Frey, but I did not say it, lest Miss Nell bolt. I could not comprehend what Lucky had held over the Major's head that led to such desperate measures.

I stuck my hands in my pockets in a gesture of resignation. "So, Lucky had something on the Major, and you made sure the Major had something on Lucky."

"Something like that."

"I believe you are an honest woman."

The smile crept back, only this time there was a tinge of sadness when she spoke. "Honest enough to know what I am." She lowered her eyes. "I am sorry for what happened to Lucky. I do not wish to see the same thing happen to you." She patted me on the cheek. "Leave the Carson Valley, John Thornton. And when you've cooled out a bit, come look me up in San Francisco, will you? I'm opening a swank little house on the Barbary Coast. I intend to name it after myself, so you will have no trouble knowing where I am. You look enough like Lucky that I am certain you must share other fine qualities." With a tilt of her head, she kissed me on the mouth, then swished back down the alleyway, leaving me to ponder the things she had said.

After Miss Nell's departure on the early stage, I had two more pieces of business. The first was to retrieve my rifle from Si Denton. His deputy, Paul Hawkins, was rummaging through a file of "wanted" papers when I came in. He studied me real hard. When he looked again at the sketches of the criminals, he seemed disappointed that he could not make me match any of the descriptions.

Si gave the lever-action to me willingly enough, and Lucky's pistol, but could not let the opportunity pass without telling me once more that I'd be better off leaving town forever—preferably the whole territory. Hawkins looked as mean as the night before, and ready to shoot me, poster or no.

I said thanks for the hospitality and went on to my other transaction. With my last double-eagle gold piece I purchased a U.S. Army mule for Kit to ride back to the sawmill.

Kit considered his long-eared mount an insult to his dignity. "Why'd you have to buy an army surplus mule?" he complained as we took off up Sawmill Road.

"All I could afford."

"That's because no fool in his right mind will own one of these beasts. You know what the U.S. brand means?" He gestured grandly at the big letters burned into the hide of the critter.

"I reckon it stands for the United States."

"Wrong!" Kit barked, shifting his seat uneasily off the creature's backbone. "Them letters mean Un-Safe at both ends!" Then he exploded, "What kinda horse trader are you anyhow? You shoulda bought me a saddle and made old Paco throw in the mule for free."

I defended myself. "I tried that. Didn't have cash enough to buy the saddle. You don't need a saddle anyhow, Kit. Didn't Mama name you after Kit Carson? Carson rode all over the west a'bareback, Indian-style, with nothing but a blanket to sit on. Follow his example, and quit grumbling."

"I'll lay odds Carson never had children," Kit muttered.

I did not let him see my amusement at his discomfort. At least his aching backside kept his mind off the Frey girl and Bernard King and the original reason he had ended up in Si's jailhouse.

In the short time since I had reacquainted myself with my youngest sibling, I had come to the conclusion that he had a lot in common with the animal he was astride. Like every jackass west of the Mississippi, Kit Thornton believed he had horse sense. Truth to tell, all he had was the inclination to kick first and ask questions later.

With Kit at my side I was confident that any attempt to get to the bottom of Lucky's murder would fail. The boy was a lit firecracker waiting to explode.

I had spent a lot of time alone over the years and did my best thinking when there was no one around for miles. This morning I needed a while to study on the situation without having to listen to Kit's complaints.

Pointing straight up to the narrow switchback trail, I said, "I'd wrap my fingers in that pup's mane if I was you. It's a steep climb. I'd hate to see you slide off his rump."

"What! I ain't going up that trail. I would not ride up that ledge with a good horse and saddle under me! I surely will not balance my life on the knife-edge spine of a four-legged troll walking a high wire."

This was exactly what I had hoped for. Kit's contrary personality had made things easy for me. I had learned to treat a mule-headed man the same as I'd corral a mule: Don't try to drive them in; just leave the gate open a crack and let them bust in. Kit was a mule who usually did just the opposite of what he was told.

"Little brother, it will take you two hours longer riding if you stick to the wagon road. Don't be so durn fool stubborn. That mule is sure-footed as a mountain goat. Ride the shortcut with me."

"On old U.S.? He'll slide and fall for certain."

"Suit yourself, little brother," I remarked, reining

Shad off the main road and letting him have his head up the steep climb.

"Don't call me little brother!" Kit bellowed.

I did not look back to see if Kit had followed until Shad had carried me most of the way up the pass. Gazing downward, I saw my brother plain as a fly on a white-linen tablecloth as the mule plodded up Sawmill Road. I figured Kit would have difficulty walking without aid by the time he reached home. I paused long enough to unsheath my repeater and scan the surrounding boulders and ledges in the canyon for any sign of ambush.

The hair on the back of my neck prickled as I spotted a thin wisp of dust rising from a ledge on the far side of the canyon wall. There are times when a man can unwind a mile of thread from what seems like a mighty small spool. A little dust might not seem like much, but it crossed my mind that a keen marksman could be the cause of it. In this case, however, the dust was nothing more than a bobcat scrambling after a varmint.

I rested Shad on that overlook for ten minutes more just to be certain Kit was not riding into trouble. I had a clear view all the way back to Genoa. If anyone had been trailing the pair of us I would have spotted him. Confident that the way was safe for Kit, unless he got thrown from the mule, I lit out toward the sawmill.

The sky got bluer the higher I rode. As the autumn mist cleared, so did some of the fog in my brain. I still had more questions than answers, but I began to see clearly what I would have to do in order to find the men who killed Lucky.

First off, there was the little matter of Major Frey. It seemed plain that he was connected somehow with Lucky. And what about the bandit named Edwards? He was supposedly Lucky's accomplice. If I could find him, perhaps I could get the truth out of him.

Lastly, there was the matter of how I could manage to leave Kit behind when I rode out again tomorrow morning. Bloodthirsty and vengeful, Kit desired nothing in the world so much as pumping lead into the heads of the nightriders who had struck him down, then hanged Lucky. "An eye for an eye and a tooth for a tooth," Kit had proclaimed when he spoke to me of that terrible night. I figured that what Kit had in mind was to make most of the men in the Carson Valley toothless and blind to avenge Lucky's death.

Sawmill meadow was quiet as I rode Shad to the corral. Smoke rose from the stovepipe. I smelled the rich aroma of venison and fresh-baked bread wafting from the cabin.

I loosened Shad's cinch, hefted the saddle onto the top rail of the corral fence, then cooled out the bay before letting him drink from the trough. About a quarter of an hour had passed and still no one had come out of the cabin to say howdy and welcome back.

Perhaps they had not heard me, although that was doubtful. I called for George. My voice echoed down the draw. After a few moments the cook-shack door groaned on its hinges and Maria stepped out.

Shading her eyes against the sun, she waved broadly, but not at me. I followed the line of her gaze to where George and the Volcanic rifle were perched high up in a nest of boulders which he called the Rock Fort.

"Come in, George," Maria called. "It's John."

The reply echoed back. "Can't come. I can see there's a bad'n coming on a mule! Gotta keep my eye on him!"

I stepped out from the corral, cupped my hands around my mouth, and hollered loud. "Don't shoot him, George! That's your Uncle Kit riding on that mule!"

As George skittered down the slope, I joined Maria on the porch. "I came the shortcut," I said to her gruffly. "Kit is on an old swayback mule. I thought I told you not to put the repeater back in George's grip where he might bag himself some two-legged critter by accident."

Hands on her hips, Maria cocked an eyebrow at me and let fly with one of her mind-your-own business looks. Not moving a step, she set me straight about the cause of George returning to sentry duty. I got the entire tale about Bernard King and Rough Elliott nearly drowning George in the water trough and killing the dog and the fact that King would surely be returning. It was Maria's intention to send the man to his eternal judgment if he ever laid a hand on her child again. The shotgun was inside where it would be handy to her if George raised a warning that danger was approaching.

She finished the account as George rushed across the field to where we stood. Maria gestured triumphantly to her son. "You see he knows his duty."

"I am justly chastised, ma'am." I doffed my hat.

"So you should be, John Thornton," she said.

George piped up, "Is that Uncle Kit on that mule? Looks like that army surplus critter Paco was trying to get rid of down at the livery. He said the old thing was costing him too much to feed. Tried to give it away but nobody'd have it. Said if anybody had a toothache the sure cure was to stand behind that mule and he'd get his dental work free. Paco said he'd shoot it, only he thought maybe somebody in a wagon train might be fool enough to buy it for ten dollars or so."

Maria's eyes narrowed with amusement at the blush I felt rising behind my whiskers. She said, "Paco gave you the mule did he?"

"Practically."

She took my arm and leaned her head against it. "I know of no one more deserving to ride that mule than dear Kit."

A considerable length of time passed before the mule arrived without Kit. It waltzed up to the water trough just pretty as you please, like as if it had lived there always. An hour after that Kit staggered in. He was walking with his legs all a-spraddle. From the look of the ground-in clay on the seat of his trousers, he had landed on a soft spot.

"Gimme a gun!" he shouted. "I'm gonna shoot it! And after that I'm gonna cut John down to a stump!"

I slipped out the back window and waited behind the outhouse. I was too full of Maria's good cooking to fight Kit. Not that I could not take him down any day of the week, but I did not fancy being punched in a full gut and losing all that good food.

Maria forbade Kit to say another word. There would be no shooting the mule or fisticuffs in her house or else. She snatched him by the ear, and told him he smelled like a hog wallow. Then when his energy was squashed, she comforted my brother with the best meal he had eaten since he got himself arrested.

I waited outside long enough for him to finish his second plateful. If he started anything with me now, I knew just where to strike in order to put him out of commission.

Not pausing for him to speak first, I reentered the place and gave Kit a big hello. "Well, little brother, I see you made it."

"No thanks to you. And don't call me little brother."

"Did you hear your old friend Bernard King was here to pay a call yesterday?"

This made Kit sit up in his chair and leave off sopping his bread in the gravy. "Here?"

George took up the recitation from there, leaving Kit

blustering and full of fight. The mule was all but forgotten.

"Let him show his face around here and I'll make him sorry for it!" Kit exclaimed.

Mindful of my need to travel fast and alone, I once more enacted my strategy for mule-headed men. "He'll be back all right." I sat down opposite Kit. "But we won't be here when he comes, worse luck. We're pulling out tomorrow morning."

Maria gave me a sharp look. Was that disappointment in her eyes?

Kit scoffed. "What is this *we*, amigo? I'm staying right here where I can meet that polecat . . ."

The bait was taken. Now I set the hook. "You are coming with me, Kit. You think I would leave you here where you might get mixed up with King and Elliott?

Maria blinked at me in disbelief. Did I intend to leave her and George to fend for themselves?

Kit said hotly, "You just don't have anything to say about it, now do you? I ain't going with you, and that's the end of it!"

In this manner I managed to make the mule want to do what I wanted. "All right, then," I said grudgingly. "But you'll have to do some work around here, then."

"Name it."

"Before I can rebuild the flume, the flow of water will have to be shut off. Climb up to the head gate on top of the cliff and plug the outlet with rocks." I figured the heavy labor would serve to reduce Kit's restless spirit . . . and for a time, I was right.

Next morning early as I set out to find Major Frey and the highwayman Edwards, it was Kit who sat perched and watching from the Rock Fort. Maria and George and the baby had protection, and I had my way. I was alone.

CHAPTER 8

Way before sunup I was off and riding back into Genoa. It was my plan not only to slip past any watchers but to turn the tables on them by showing up where least expected. Besides that, I figured the Major was a methodical man—a creature of habit—and I meant to turn his habits to my advantage.

Behind the barbershop was a bathhouse. In point of fact, it was a lean-to shed stuck on the back of the one-room frame building, but it had an outside door that could be bolted from the inside.

I hammered on the door of the tonsorial establishment and roused the little Mexican fella who operated the place. I could hear him grumping in Spanish as he arose from his cot in the corner of the room and shuffled across the floor. "Bueños dias, amigo," I greeted his sleepy face, "I am in need of a hot bath and a shave and a haircut."

"Come back later, señor," was the reply. "The shop, she is closed."

"It's worth ocho reales if I can get cleaned up right away," I offered. "I need to look sharp to meet my gal."

I calculated this to be an irresistible combination. The Spanishers are incurable romantics, so that was one appeal. The other ingredient in my persuasion was that I had offered him eight Mexican coins that were the equivalent of a dollar for services that usually traded for two bits. "Come in, come in, señor," he agreed, bowing and smiling. He put a white smock on over his undershirt and bustled around setting a tub of water to boil on the bathhouse wood stove.

"One more thing," I added, heading toward the back room. "I like a good, long wash to soak off all the real estate I'm wearing, sabe? Don't be trying to sell my bath water before I'm finished with it."

"Oh no, señor," the short shearmaster agreed. "It is yours for as long as you wish."

I poured a bucketful of hot water into the tin washtub and mixed it with cool rainwater from a barrel mounted on the wall. I swirled it around from time to time so Señor Gomez would know that I had not drowned or anything, but mostly I sat and waited.

Another customer showed up while I studied the shop through a knothole. I thought about striking up a conversation about Frey and King and Rough Elliott, to see if he knew anything, but when you go out to hunt grizzlies, you should not waste time chasing rabbits. The man, who must have been a banker by his clothing, got his shave and his hair dressed with lime water and then took his leave.

The next two men who came along looked and smelled like they needed bathing, but that was not what they were after. Seems they had spent too much time in the company of tarantula juice the night previous. Señor Gomez had a renowned spider bite cure for just such a need. Those boys must have had heads in terrible need of shrinking back to their hat sizes, on account of they watched the barber mix raw eggs, cayenne pepper, vinegar, and bicarbonate of soda into a frothy, slimy mess, and they each took a slug anyhow. They even muttered thanks before staggering back outside.

This sideshow was all very amusing, but not profitable for me, until the fourth patron showed and it was the Major, come at last. I held back until he had his beard all wrapped in a hot towel, and then I called out to Gomez. "Hey, señor, you got any seegars? I want a smoke with my soak."

When the barber replied that he had no cigars, I told him I'd give him another fifty cents to fetch me some. I heard him ask permission from the Major, who grunted his consent, then the door opened and closed and the Major and I were alone.

A tan, knee-length frock coat hung on a brass hook near the door. An oval of the Major's face could be glimpsed in the center of the swathing. Below this he wore a gray plaid waistcoat and gray-checked trousers. I came out of the back room scrubbing my hair as if it were wet.

"Howdy," I said.

"How do," he acknowledged without seeming to know who I was. "What brand do you smoke? I have a couple here in my pocket if you'd like one."

"No, thanks," I said. "I don't believe in taking things under false pretenses."

His eyes widened at that from their drowsy, relaxed condition. "What do you mean by that?" he inquired, starting to sit upright. I put my palm in the center of his chest and pushed him back down.

"I'm John Thornton," I said, "and I mean to ask you some questions."

"I do not conduct business from a barber's chair," he said bluntly. "You may come to my office . . ."

"This suits me fine," I said, leaning on the buttons of his waistcoat with the heel of my hand. "We won't get interrupted here."

"Are you threatening me?" he demanded. "If so, I'll have you arrested."

I shook my head and laughed. "Are you hiding something, Major? I don't have to threaten, and you have nothing to fret about if you can tell me truthfully what you know."

That settled him some. He could tell that bluster would not make me leave, and he could read in my eyes that I was deadly serious. "All right," he agreed. "Ask."

"What do you know about my brother's death?"

Shrugging, the Major answered, "No more than anyone else. Your brother met his death at the hands of men who believed him to be guilty of murder and other crimes. He had been accused of thieving, as well as harboring criminals. Most folks say he got what was coming to him."

"Is that what you say?"

Weighing his words carefully, the Major replied, "I won't deny that we had our differences when it came to business. He never forgave me for besting him at the sawmill business or for winning large sums from him at cards."

"You beat Lucky?" I said, sounding amazed. "I never knew him to lose unless he meant to."

"Maybe the game was not to his liking." This was a thinly veiled way to accuse Lucky of being a cheat without really using those words. I don't know if the Major said it to get a rise out of me, but I made no response, and he continued, "You know he threatened my life?"

"What was that?"

The Major nodded vigorously as if he was anxious to convince me that he had been wronged. "I heard from Lute Olds that Lucky said he'd pay cash money if someone would kill me."

Señor Gomez returned right then with a fistful of cigars which he extended to me. I flipped him the quarters. "Give the cigars to the Major," I said. "I owe him something for the conversation. By the way, Major," I concluded. "There is just one thing. I intend to keep looking till I find out the truth, and then heaven help you if you lied to me."

"Is that a threat?" he repeated.

"Nope. No matter what some other black-hearted scoundrels may think, it's high time that the rule of law really came to this territory. I'll see that the proper authorities take care of it, and you'll get the fair trial that Lucky never saw."

Si gave me a description of the man named Edwards. The paper on him from the Placerville killing described him as thin, two inches below six feet in height, with light brown hair and beard. Most importantly, he was said to have a notch in one ear from an old gunshot wound. "But even if you catch up with him, what will it prove?" Si asked me. "Do you think he'll confess to murdering Gordier and put his own neck in a noose?"

"No," I said slowly, "but I have to start somewhere if I'm ever going to untangle this knot. Somebody tried to connect a man wanted for murder with my brother. He may know why. Besides, Si, you wouldn't object if I brought in a wanted man, would you?"

Shaking his head to show he thought I was crazy, Si wished me luck and slapped Shad on the rump to speed me out of town. Bernard King watched me go from the steps of the Frey hotel as I passed that way. It was clear that a lot of folks were very interested in my comings and goings.

I had given out to Si and others that I was headed up to the Honey Lake country, the same region as the last reported whereabouts of Edwards. But that was just to put any followers off my trail.

In actual fact, my plan was to ride out north, then double back up a canyon till I could circle around to Hope Valley to the south and west of Genoa. I was minded again to see if I could locate Snowshoe Thompson. He knew all the gossip in those parts, and if anyone matching Edwards's looks was anywhere around, he would know of it. More than that, if one of the vigilantes had let slip a single word of their participation in my brother's hanging, Snowshoe would know.

My scheme evidently worked. A plume of dust behind me on the road north showed at least one pursuer, but my sudden swerve behind a barn-sized boulder went unremarked. Shad and I made our way up and out of the Carson Valley, looped behind the Old Emigrant Trail, and soon found ourselves again at Snowshoe's place.

This time I was in luck. A trickle of smoke rising from the stovepipe of his cabin and a shirt and two pair of unmentionables drying on a rock were evidence that the letter carrier was at home.

The tall, lean frame of the man straightened up from bending over a washtub when he heard the hoofbeats of my approach. He shielded his eyes for a minute and then waved me to come on up to his home.

"John Thornton!" the long-bearded Thompson exclaimed. His accent made my first name sound like Yon, and I was pleased that he recognized me.

The inside of Showshoe's home was just as I remembered it, but then it looked like hundreds of other log cabins, including one I had built myself once. It was a single room with a door that faced south and a fireplace built against the solid rock face that formed the north wall. On the hearth were coffeepot, fry pan, and Dutch oven. Leaning in a nearby corner were the eight-foot-long, flat, wooden snowshoes which gave Thompson his nickname. Since winter can arrive in the Sierras as early as October, it would not be long before he pressed them into service again.

A table occupied the center of the room. Its top was embellished with fanciful curlicues by Snowshoe's jack-knife, the result of many a lonely night's carving. On it rested most of his worldly goods: tin plates and cups, bottles of molasses and vinegar, boxes of salt and sugar, and a well-thumbed Bible, re-covered in buckskin. Dried strips of meat hanging from the rafters completed the domestic arrangements.

"A bad business 'bout your brotter," Showshoe began. "Very bad indeed. You vill find who done it, yah?"

"Why I'm here," I agreed. "Hoping you could point me in the right direction."

Showshoe stroked his chest-length beard and pondered. "It is strange," he said. "I don't hear notting. Oh sure, I hear vat dey say your brother did, but no von brags about his killing."

I was disappointed, but a cold trail could warm up sudden with the right turning. "What about Edwards?" I asked. "Who told you he was up in the Honey Lake country?"

Showshoe thought a moment. "It vas a gambler fellow. King, I tink his name is."

I nodded. Snowshoe had deliberately been fed the wrong information. King had known that Thompson's report would send Si Denton on a wild goose chase. "Lucky was supposed to have this Edwards as an accomplice. Have you seen anyone matching his appearance?"

The mail carrier looked puzzled. "Vhy you tink he be around here?"

"Just a hunch," I said. "I think Si Denton and the posse were deliberately sent away from Genoa in the wrong direction. Since I don't think Edwards would go back toward Placerville, the only direction left is this way, toward Border Ruffian Pass."

Showshoe said nothing as he stood and went to his cot. Reaching beneath it, he produced a leather pouch and a pair of clay pipes. "It makes sense, vat you say," he agreed. "I need to smoke and tink on it some. You vant to join me?"

I shook my head. "I passed a covey of quail in a draw a ways back," I said. "The least I can do is get us fresh meat for supper." I wondered if Snowshoe had guessed that his unknowing role in the deception had been part of my brother's capture and hanging.

His head already wreathed in a blue haze of smoke, Snowshoe waved me toward the door. It was plain from the faraway expression on his face that he was casting up Edward's portrait alongside men he had met in his travels.

After a supper of fried quail, Snowshoe reared back on his bench and screwed up one eye. This was a sure sign that he was about to deliver either information, innuendo, or advice; Snowshoe dispensed all three with equal enthusiasm.

"I gif your man Edwards some tought," he said, scratching a match on the plank floor and lighting an after-dinner pipe. "And dere is someone who could be him. Mind you," he cautioned, "I do not say he is de one, only he could be."

"Whereabouts?"

"As you say, it vas down in Border Ruffian country, across de pass at Bone's Toll station. Man name Tick runs it now. Anyvay, a feller who looks like your man sat in a corner by himself."

"Did he act suspicious or nervous?"

"No, but he kept playing vith his hair, like a girl vith

pigtails, pulling on it so." Snowshoe demonstrated what he meant by yanking on his own graying locks.

It was a far piece to Bone's Toll station—a good two-day ride and a chilly one at eight thousand feet above sea level and the turn of the season past. It was not a journey to make lightly, especially to leave Maria and the others alone to no purpose. Snowshoe was waiting for my response. "Lot of brown-haired medium- sized men grow their hair long," I said. "Anything more?"

"Yah," Snowshoe agreed. "I hear a stage driver ask dis feller's name just as Tick trow down a bowl of beans. Dis man jump vhen de bowl tump on de table." Snowshoe's eyes were sparkling. He was plainly spinning out his news for all he was worth and enjoying the suspense. "Den he sputters like Tick's coffee vas choking him, vich I do not say is not possible . . ."

"Snowshoe," I warned, "get on with it."

"Dat is all," he concluded, looking offended at my lack of enthusiasm. "He says his name is Ed . . . Ed Coombs, but I swear he start to say someting else. And Yon." Now Snowshoe's kindly eyes showed concern. "I hear someting else at Bone's. I hear dat Indians been raiding and stealing cattle down dat vay. You vatch yourself."

CHAPTER 9

Above Snowshoe's cabin at Diamond Springs the road forked into a choice between west and south. West lay the route through the Carson Pass toward Placerville over which I had lately come. South continued the Old Emigrant Trail through Hope, Faith, and Charity Valleys, past Blue Lake, and up over Border Ruffian Pass.

Bidding Snowshoe good-bye with thanks, I directed my course southward, up from the country of sagebrush and rocky gullies into God's own landscape. Reading the signs, I could tell that someone driving a small herd of cattle had passed that same way not long before.

There surely was some beautiful scenery that direction. Just beyond Charity Valley I came across a long slope covered in lodgepole pines and red cedars. Shad and I rode out upon a promontory to survey a big meadow, full two hundred acres in space, spread out there below us. The stream through its middle was winding and bubbled over ripples that just begged a man to hunt him up a cane pole and some worms. The course of the creek was bordered with quaking aspens, their fluttering leaves turning all golden yellow. From my point of rock the aspen trees looked like thirty-foot-tall flames in both shape and color.

The road ahead was plain enough, but I took advantage of the high ground to survey the distance. Though I could see no fumes, I caught a whiff of campfire smoke. Shad must have noticed it, too, because I saw an interested set to his head. When I followed his gaze, I spotted it at last—a covered wagon mostly sheltered by the overhanging boughs of a cedar on the far side of the meadow.

Back in the days of the great westering of the '40s and the Gold Rush stampede in '49 and '50, this had been a well-known route into El Dorado and points south. There were stretches where the trail crossed hardpan rock that was worn into ruts by the passage of the wheels. Scarified trees sported bark calluses that would forever show the rubbing of countless hubs. But what with regular stage service by way of the Carson Pass, few new arrivals ventured down this way anymore. Mostly the Old Emigrant Trail was traveled by folks who already had some reason to be heading down to the Calaveras country.

Whoever this party was, they had made a precious late start of it. Camping in the back of beyond this time of year was an invitation to wintering over without planning to do so. Those left from the Donner folks could tell of such an experience. Still, there was no sign of snow in the sky yet, and these travelers should be all right.

I shaped my course toward their layout, hoping for a friendly cup of coffee and a word.

Viewed from a couple hundred yards distant, there seemed to be no one about the emigrant camp. What with all the possibilities for rustling up mule deer and brook trout, that was not too surprising. Something bothered me about the setup, though, even if I could not put my finger on it. The rig looked well-cared for, its canvas cover made of whole cloth and not patchwork. Just beyond it, even further hidden by the shadows of the trees, was the remains of the campfire I had smelled. "Hello the camp!" I hollered as I drew nearer. Politeness called for such an announcement, but personal safety was another factor; newcomers to the West tended to be nerved up when it came to Indians and outlaws. After George had come near to parting my hair with a bullet, I really did not care to give anyone else a turn.

In reality there was precious little for travelers to fret about. Cholera, accidents from tomfoolery with firearms, and drownings had far and away accounted for more deaths on the trail in one year than all the hostile attacks put together. Add in the tenderfeet who had gone to glory by arguing with long-haired whiskey drinkers, and Indians as a threat were downright overrated.

The local tribes, mostly Washoes, Paiutes, and a sprinkling of Miwoks, had never done more than drive off herd beasts and such. The last Indian raid on a mining camp had been clear back in 1853 and had brought fearful reprisals on innocent and guilty alike.

Coming upon a newcomer encampment churned all these thoughts in my mind. I wondered if they had also heard tell of new Indian troubles and if they were lying low and spying on me because of it. "Hello the camp," I called again, though I was nought but a hundred yards away now and they must certainly have heard my arrival. "I'm friendly."

It was then that what had bothered me became plain: Not only were there no people about, neither were there animals. Where were the oxen or mules that had pulled these wagons to this lonely spot? Even if their human masters were out foraging, the critters should have been grazing in the nearby grassland. That was precisely the reason why a traveling party would stop in that place. For that matter, where were the rest of the cow critters whose fresh tracks I had seen back up the way? I should have caught up with them by now.

Shad snorted and drew up sharp. His ears were pricked forward, but they flicked toward the rear and the skin of his neck twitched. I have never been the easily agitated sort myself, but I had learned from long experience that paying attention to animal signals can save your hide. Shad's timely warning of a nearby grizzly mama and cub had early on convinced me that he was trustworthy.

With the ring of trees around me and the open meadow behind, I was too easy a target for an unseen watcher.

Without giving any notice of my intentions, I swung Shad's head toward a big pine tree and put in the spurs.

The bay covered the distance in a pair of bounds, one of which took him over a four-foot-high fallen log. I slipped off his back and shucked the repeater from its scabbard in the same motion.

From behind that tree trunk I surveyed the encampment with a different eye. Too silent and too still could mean a trap, but for who? No one knew I was coming this way, or so I hoped.

A flash of crimson caught my attention from a spot beyond the wagon. Something was nearly hidden in a clump of dark red manzanita, but whatever this was had a brighter color than the bark of the shrub.

Leaving Shad ground-tied back of the log, I circled to the left, ducking from tree to tree and looking over my shoulder real regular. No sounds came to me, and no gunshot rang out when I took my slouch hat off my head and raised it up on a branch. The back of my neck prickled, and I shivered once, but I went on toward that clump of manzanita just the same.

There was a man lying in the brush. He was dead. What I had spotted as a gleam of scarlet was his blood-covered shirt. A pair of arrows pierced his back between the suspender cords holding his striped britches. He would never see his twenty-fifth birthday.

I found his partner in a gully about twenty yards away. Much of the same age, he also was shot in the back. When I turned him over, his chest had another wound just over his heart.

These were Paiute arrows by the look of them. My read on what happened was that the two men had been sitting peaceable, drinking coffee around their campfire, when a party of savages jumped them. From the fact that neither man had weapons to hand suggested that the Indians had approached and pretended to be friendly before bushwhacking and slaughtering the pair. The second feller must have been a regular bull for strength I guessed. His chest wound had bled considerable and yet he had been able to run off a ways before his attacker put an arrow in his back to finish him. There was not even much blood on the man's back, him having almost bled to death before.

It took me the rest of the afternoon to bury the pair there under the big cedar. I committed their souls to God, reflecting all the while that if I had come along sooner, maybe the Volcanic lever-action and I could have prevented this. 'Course, if I had gotten my wish to share their coffee and fire, I might have shared in their death as well.

I found papers that told me their names and a small Bible given to one of them with the inscription *Good Luck Out West, But Come Back To Me Soon*. It was signed, *Sally*.

The documents and the Bible I tucked in my saddlebag. I would try to see that they got sent back to Sally. It was as far back to Genoa as it was on to Bone's and either would do to report the deaths, so I decided to press ahead. When the spoor of the stolen cattle turned aside from the Emigrant Road and into a side canyon, I marked the turning to show a posse later, but made no move to follow.

I met no other travelers between the site of the killings and Bone's Toll Station. Whether this was because of an already spreading fear of Indian attacks or not I could not know.

Bone's was an unappealing wide spot in the road to say the least. Established at the height of the Gold Fever immigration to collect fees for road maintenance, it also served as a meal stop for man and beast. But nothing better described its character than its nickname: Old Dry Bones. The roof was sway-backed like a broken-down horse and the three remaining props holding up the porch were trying to run away south. The interior smelled as if all the chinks in the log walls had been stuffed with rancid bear fat, which they probably had.

The current proprietor was called Mr. Thick, and this was equally as good a description as it was a name. He was almost as big around as he was tall and had a floor-length apron that came up under his armpits. It seemed to me that the apron was the same as I had noted on a previous owner some years earlier, but then one streak of axle grease looks much like another.

Mister Thick invited me to turn Shad into the corral with two other horses and a brace of mules. One of those horses, a palomino, had the look of a champion about him: long, ground-covering legs and big hocks for drive. "Fine looking animal," I commented. "Yours?" Thick muttered something in reply and suggested that we join the guests inside. I grabbed his elbow outside the door to have a word before entering. "You know about the Indian trouble?" I asked.

"Know about it?" he sputtered. "If I had that Snowshoe Thompson here I'd wring his scrawny neck! His wild stories have got everybody panicked clean back to Salt Lake! Ain't nobody crossing this trail no more, and what he says is all tall tales!"

"Lower your voice," I muttered. "It's real. I just buried two men the other side of Border Ruffian Pass. They were shot full of Paiute arrows and their stock run off."

I looked to see if Thick would turn pale at the news, but beneath three days beard and a layer of other substances, it was impossible to tell. "You figger they'll come this way?"

"I doubt it," I said. "They got what they were after. But somebody needs to know and get up a posse."

Thick nodded. "I'll get word to the sheriff, but I don't know how many volunteers he'll find."

"One more thing. Is there a man name of Coombs here abouts?"

Thick's eyes narrowed and he studied some high

mare's tail clouds before he replied. "Nope, don't ring no bells."

"Brown-haired man, about your height, with a notch missing out of one ear."

"That don't bring nobody to mind neither. Why? What's he done?"

"Did I say he had done something?"

That ended the conference. I took my gear off the fence rail and entered the station.

If I had thought to find Coombs, or rather, Edwards, waiting for me inside I was mistaken. Instead there was a troupe of actors and actresses from a traveling company. They were on their way from the mining towns of Calaveras to winter quarters in the Carson Valley when their wagon had chosen this spot to bust a wheel. Three men and three ladies comprised the company, and none could possibly have been Edwards.

They were yammering something fierce, picking on their leader mostly, as if he had personally caused their misfortune. That tall, white-haired man with the aristocratic nose was trying to soothe them, saying that it would only mean a delay of a day or so, but they were as unimpressed with the comforts offered by Bone's Station as I was.

I settled myself in a corner of the room and pulled my hat brim down a bit. Thick shuffled around the room, ladling plates of beans out of a cauldron on the wood stove. When one of the ladies complained that her dish was none too clean, Thick graciously took it up, wiped it on his apron, and set it back down in front of her. I noted that she seemed to lose her appetite after that.

After getting everyone served, Thick said he would go see to the horses, and out he went. I counted to ten, picked up the repeater, and then slipped out the back door.

As I had guessed, after tossing a few bundles of grass into the corral, Thick headed off into the woods, away from the station. He kept looking back over his shoulder, but I had enough woodcraft in me to always be behind cover when he did so.

About a hundred yards across a clearing there was a lean-to built against a rock. Thick looked around once more, then slipped inside. A minute later he emerged again and retraced his steps, with me watching all the while from behind a screen of willows.

After he passed, I levered in a shell and cocked the hammer back. The lean-to had no windows and only one door, which I approached as soft as a whisper. From inside I could hear rustling and clattering, as the sounds made by someone in a hurry to pack up.

I kicked open the door with the Volcanic held waist-high. A medium-sized man dropped the satchel into which he was stuffing his shirts and stooped toward a Colt's Baby Dragoon pistol that was lying on the floor.

"I wouldn't touch that just now, if I was you," I warned.

"Who are you, and what do you want?" the man asked in a squeaky voice.

"I'm the Federal ear inspector on my rounds," I said. "And I'm here to see yours. Now flip that hair back."

Reluctantly, but complying in the face of the rifle's persuasion, he did so. The top of his left ear was shy about a half inch of its circumference. "Coombs," I confirmed, "or Edwards. Which is it?"

"It was self-defense," he argued. "It was him or me. What else was I supposed to do? Let him kill me?"

"Pipe down," I ordered. "My name is Thornton, and I'm taking you back to Genoa."

"Genoa?" he asked with a puzzled look. "Don't you mean Placerville?"

"I know that you're wanted in Placerville, but this matter concerns my brother's lynching over in Carson Valley."

"You're gonna shoot me in the woods!"

I shook my head. "Not if you don't try to run," I said. "I want the truth out of you, and then you'll be turned over to the authorities, but I have no plan to act like them who executed my brother. Now get your things."

CHAPTER 10

It was in my mind, now that I had located Edwards, to take him back to Genoa for Si Denton to hold. Then I would send word for the territorial marshall to come, even if I had to go to Salt Lake City to fetch him myself.

I had Edwards back away from the pistol while I stooped and picked it up. Stuffing the Colt in my waistband, I motioned with the rifle for him to get on with his packing.

Edwards stuffed the satchel with his belongings, including a tintype of a gray-haired woman dressed all in black with a high collar. Her expression would have clabbered milk, but Edwards was blubbering when he gazed at it. "My own dear mother," he whimpered. "She warned me not to come out West. She said I'd fall into evil companions and dire trials, and she was right. Oh, how I hate to bring this shame on her when she finds out."

This was not at all what I had expected. The man I thought I was trailing was supposed to be a hardened criminal who had killed at least twice and had no feelings of remorse. What was the game here?

"A little late for regrets now," I said coldly. "I don't know about the Placerville shooting, but killing Gordier in cold blood to steal his cattle . . ."

"But I didn't kill Gordier!" Edwards protested. He threw up his hands in a gesture of appeal and stepped toward me. I waved him back with a warning wag of the Volcanic. "I wouldn't harm that old Frenchman. He did me nothing but good!"

Seeing as how he was disposed to talk, I was inclined to let him. Even if I had to sort the truth from the fiction later, I might learn something. Edwards struck me as the breed of man who will do anything to save his own skin. He might even spill what he knew about someone else.

"All right," I said. "I'm listening."

Edwards sat down on top of the single threadbare blanket that covered his cot. He looked at me with a pitiful, pleading kind of stare. "It was in a saloon in Placerville," he began. "There was a girl and a man name of Snelling . . ."

"I don't care about Placerville," I reminded him. "What happened after?"

It was getting dark outside, and the inside of the shack was steeping in gloom. "I got away by stealing a horse," he admitted. "I thought they were gonna lynch me without a trial!"

"It's been known," I said dryly. "Go on."

"This was a race horse, see? Bald Hornet. Ever hear of him? Fastest horse I ever seen, I . . ."

"Friend," I said abruptly. "You are sorely trying my patience, which is already in short supply. Now either get to the point, or I might change my mind and haul you back to them Placervillians."

Swallowing hard, Edwards wiped his stubble-covered face. "I distanced the posse, and when I come to Hope Valley, I hid out with Gordier. He took me in, see, on account of I knew him when I first come West. Said he'd hide me till the trouble blew over. You know I didn't kill him! He was my friend!"

"So what happened?" Edwards cast a look toward the door, a quick glance that told me he was ready to bolt. "Don't even think it," I cautioned. "You can't outrun a lead slug."

That settled his hash a mite, and he continued. "One day late last spring, the old man sent me out to check on a calf. Said he thought a lion had got it. When I come back, he was dead!"

"How do you mean?"

Edwards fairly screamed, "Dead, I tell you! There was blood all over, and the ax that killed him still lying on the floor. I picked it up . . ." Edwards shuddered all over like a man would with a fatal chill. No matter what else he might be concocting, this emotion was genuine. "That's when they showed up."

"Who's they?"

"I don't know their names! A gent, a big man, and

another smaller feller. Got the drop on me. Said I'd hang for certain. I tried to reason with them. Told them what happened, same as I'm telling you. They said it wouldn't wash, that I was good as hanged unless . . ."

"Unless what?"

But the discharge of words had halted as quick as it started. Edwards had gone from being unable to control the gush of his tale to a stony silence.

"Unless what?" I repeated.

"I'm not saying anymore," he vowed.

"Why not?"

"Not till you get the marshall and the judge. I don't want to die. Not by lynch mob and not by those men neither!"

"Just tell me what you know about them." Edwards shook his head, and I was sorely tempted to crack him across the teeth with the barrel of the repeater, but I refrained. "Then get up!" I said roughly. "We're going back to Genoa now, tonight."

Edwards marched out the door ahead of me like a man resigned to his fate, like a man in control of himself. Like a man who had an ace up his sleeve.

The chunk of stovewood that hit me in the back of the head might have been a whole giant redwood falling out of the forest for the effect it had on me. The rifle flew out of my hands, and I pitched forward. Just before I hit the ground I had time to call myself a few choice names for being so stupid. Edwards had been playing for time until his accomplice arrived. And I had fallen for it.

A woman's heart-shaped face, framed by cascades of dark ringlets, was hovering over my head when I came to my senses again. "Maria?" I murmured hopefully, rubbing my hand across my eyes in a futile effort to brush the fog away.

"No, more's the pity," the lady answered. "From the tone of your voice I'd say you must care for her a whole lot." I struggled to sit upright, and made it about halfway before a lightning bolt ripped through my skull and I sank back with a moan. "Easy," the woman cautioned. "Don't get in a hurry. You've had a blow that should have cracked your head like an egg. Tess has gone to fetch the men to help you into the station. I'm Lavinia."

"Coombs . . . I mean, Edwards . . . where did he go?"

My vision clearing at last, I could see that my words made no sense to Lavinia. "I don't know who you mean, unless it's the fella who took out of here with Thick."

"They're both gone?"

Lavinia nodded. "We were just beginning to wonder where our portly host had gotten off to when he and the other came tearing out of the woods. They wouldn't stop to answer any questions, just saddled up and took off. Knocked Tyrone down—that's our manager—when he tried to find out what was up."

So that was who had clobbered me. Edwards had played me like a hooked fish until Thick returned to the cabin. That explained why Edwards had talked so loud at times—to let his accomplice know to get ready. I struggled to my feet, with no more than a few Independence Day fireworks going off in my head. I needed to get on their trail and fast.

The white-haired man came puffing up the path about then. With him was a blonde gal and another man. "What is it, Lavinia? Bandits? Did that cursed proprietor flee and leave us to our fate?"

Lavinia, who seemed calmer and more sensible than the rest, answered by pointing to the knot on the back of my head. "It seems that Mister Thick and another man have waylaid Mister . . . Mister?"

"Thornton," I supplied.

"Thornton," she repeated. "And then they decamped."

"Leaving us undefended?" squeaked the blonde, much to the evident embarrassment of the two men.

"There's nothing much to be afraid of now," I said. "Thick has just helped a man wanted for murder, so I'd say the danger is gone. Just show that you are wary, and the Indians won't bother you."

"Indians!" all of them exclaimed.

I had forgotten that they did not know about the killings, so I had to explain. This undid all the reassuring I had tried to do. "Where's your broken wheel?" I asked, trying to get back to practical considerations.

"Thick sent it to a blacksmith down in Tamarack,"

Tyrone answered. "He promised to have it back tomorrow."

I nodded. Tamarack was a village just a few miles down the road. "You'll be safe here tonight. Tell the blacksmith what I said, then you can either wait here for the posse to escort you through, or turn back the way you came."

"What about you?" Lavinia wanted to know.

"I'm going after Thick and the other man."

There was some argument about my condition and the sense of riding at night, but I was determined not to give them too long a head start. With luck Shad and I might catch up to them by sunup.

"I'm afraid," Lavinia said, "that they've stolen your horse."

Shad was gone, and so was the palomino. Thick had opened the corral gate and turned out the last horse and the mules. His intent was to prevent any possibility of my following, but he had been in too big a hurry to do the job right. The critters had only run off as far as the meadow behind the station.

I found a sack of grain and rattled some in a tin cup. Soon enough I had a bridle on the remaining horse. He was old enough to vote, by the look of him, and not built for speed, but he was sound. Fortunately for me, the fugitives had not thought to take my saddle or rifle with them, so I rigged up my gear and headed out into the night.

Lavinia had told me that the pair of renegades had galloped away east, back toward Border Ruffian Pass. There was a full moon rising over the crest of the Sierras, and I was soon making good time.

Some might question my decision to follow at night, but I knew the country roundabout; there were precious few places where a man could break new trail through the brush without leaving a sign that stood out like an old man with a young wife.

What's more, I had me a secret weapon. This unexpected advantage was actually because they had stolen Shad. The wind was coming from the southwest, directly behind me. That circumstance meant that whenever I drew close to them Shad would smell me coming, and when he did, he would try to get back to me or give me a call of welcome.

All in all, I felt pretty sanguine about my chances of overtaking them, despite the lump on my head. What would take place when we met up was something else again. That they would fight was a certainty, but it was equally clear that I needed Edwards alive. Who were the men who had confronted him at Gordier's? Was he really framed for the killing, or had that all been part of the ruse? What did he know about my brother?

After a couple hours of steady riding I was crossing the boulder-strewn reaches of Petrified Valley. Here I was near the headwaters of rivers that flowed down into the

Calaveras country. In the glow of the moon's orb sailing high, the shadows on the land were sharp as daytime. Every ancient petrified tree stump had skull-like features and deep-set eye sockets. It reminded me that the old Spaniards had named the region Calaveras—Calvary— for the bones of all the dead Indians they discovered there, unburied a century after some forgotten quarrel.

The landscape around me was littered with fallen trees and antique stumps long since more rock than timber and eerily frozen between life and death. It had an evil, unnatural feel, as if under some long-abiding judgment of the Lord. Pretty soon some of the ossified spars of the vanished forest became Lot's wife and all her kin after the destruction of Sodom.

I spurred the old horse and jogged on. His hooves clattered over some loose stones. Then, amid the sharp rattle of the rocks, I thought I heard Shad whinny. It was a soft sound, still a ways off, but unmistakably his call.

Throwing a loop of lead rope around Lot's dearly departed, I shook myself out of spooky tales and back to practical concerns. Up ahead of me was a brace of men with at least a pistol and maybe more weaponry. If I did not want to become part of this eternal graveyard, I needed caution.

From stub to boulder to heap of stones I dashed, always trying to look more like part of the shadowy countryside than a living intruder. Popping out from behind a granite-hard tree and flinging myself into a gully, I made unintentional acquaintance with a skunk.

Luckily for me I made my exit before he could load and fire.

There was a broad expanse of open ground just ahead of me. For a good thirty yards there would be no cover, unless I backtracked and circled around, but that would cost precious time. Time was not something I was willing to waste either. If I was concerned about walking into their fire, I was also worried they would hear my approach and decide to flee instead of fight. I did not want this chase to go on much longer.

While I was still debating what to do, Shad whinnied again. Silently I urged him to be quiet and not give the game away. In the meantime I had reached my decision, and on my belly I slithered forward, thankful that the nights were now cold enough to have driven the rattlers underground; or so I hoped.

I had crossed perhaps half of the exposed area when I heard a footfall and then another, coming directly toward me. I froze in place, sliding the repeater forward a silent inch at a time.

The rifle was still not where I wanted it when the noise of someone treading on the rocks came again, almost close enough to touch. A long shadow stretched out across the stone table and reached for me as if seeking to grab me.

I rolled over to free the lever-action and snapped up to my knees. "Freeze," I warned. "I've got you dead to rights!" I was hoping a little bluff would make up for my bad position; it would scarcely make it worse.

Without a reply the shadow and the footsteps came forward again, falling across me there as if the weight of the darkness could pin me to the moonlight-drenched scene.

It was Shad. Obedient to my unspoken request, he had stopped calling for me, but he had still ambled forward to locate me.

I stood up slowly, aware of the fact that a cunning enemy might play just such a trick: send my horse out to find me and turn the tables on my scheme. I had not thought either Thick or Edwards to be that clever.

I rose to my feet and slid my hand up the stirrup leather, using the horse's bulk to shield my movements. I had just reached full upright with my hand on the cantle of the saddle when my fingers encountered something wet and sticky. Even by moonlight it was not difficult to interpret—it was blood.

Shad and I traveled together across the mesa. I retraced his route as best I was able, judging by the direction from which he had appeared and the compass point from which I first heard him call. It took no great trail-craft to know that foul play was afoot. But whose blood was it? Did it belong to Edwards or to Thick or to an unknown? And who had spilled the blood? Was it the Paiutes again, an accident, treachery, or something else altogether?

These thoughts were a mental exercise that did nothing to relieve the tension of the hour. Any combination of them might still spell trouble for me. If it was possible, I slunk forward even more cautiously than before.

Shad stopped for no reason I could see or hear. He seemed reluctant to go forward, and a ripple of nervousness passed over his hide. He was once again giving me plenty of warning, but about what?

A low groan came from the darkness ahead of me. Almost a sigh, it was a sound of such weariness and misery that I was half inclined to credit the Indian tales of what baneful spirits inhabited that ridge. But not many ghosts call for water, and if it was a Paiute spook being canny, well, it also spoke English.

"Water," the weak voice croaked again, and in that moment I recognized the pitch as Edwards's. It still might be a trap, so I dropped into a crouch and surveyed the surroundings.

Even in the dark some things look natural and proper. What I was scanning for was something out of place—a shape that did not fit.

Just ahead of me a pair of petrified logs lay tumbled together. The moon illuminated the space between their trunks, right up to the point where they crossed. Exposed to view just ahead of that shade was a tree limb . . . except that it looked wrong. It was bent funny, and it did not sparkle like the mineral-laden surface of the fossilized timber.

And then it moved.

Edwards was gut shot when I found him, and nearing the end of his string. I fetched my canteen, knowing that nothing I could do would postpone his death. At best I could ease his passing.

After he had taken a gulp of water, he moaned, "Thick did this to me! I told him I wouldn't talk . . . don't shoot! I'll keep still! Don't!"

He was raving in his agony, but when he quieted, I urged him to make his peace with his Maker. "I can't pray!" he cried. "Help me, stranger! Help me pray! I betrayed a man to his death, and I'm lost . . . lost!"

What a dilemma was here before me. The one source of information about my brother's fate was in my hands, and he was dying . . . might go West between ragged breaths. How I wanted to wring what he knew from him . . . to threaten him with hell's fire if he did not instantly confess all he knew!

But I did not. It was not because of some innate goodness of my own, but purely because we all have to face the terrors of the dark hour. To see Edwards gripped with horror was to look down the road at my own mortality.

And so I spoke of the thief on the cross—a murderer and a thief justly condemned and punished. That man, brought to the very edge of the abyss, was accepted as forgiven at the moment he asked it.

And so did Edwards ask forgiveness, and I trust that God will pardon me for eavesdropping on his confession. "I repent of my wickedness. They told me I'd hang if I did not lie for them," he groaned. "They told me what to say, and I did it."

"Who?" I urged gently.

"Thornton. I lied about Thornton. I said he put me up to killing Gordier. Then they let me escape."

"Who?" I goaded him again. "Who put you up to it?"

Edwards lurched against the frozen tree trunk, and bloody foam appeared on his lips. When he spoke again it was with great difficulty. "Penrod . . . and Olds," he said at last.

This was not at all what I was expecting. "Who?" I asked again, dumbfounded.

"Said I had to convince Penrod . . . Olds . . . others . . ." he mumbled, his voice trailing off to a faint whisper.

"Who made you?"

"Frey," he sighed, the feeble word trailing downward like a thread of spider silk drifting on the breeze.

"Why?" I demanded. "What was the cause?"

But in the fragment of time between his last reply and my question, Edwards was already in another place, before another questioner.

There was no point in following Thick any further that night. I had found what I had sought. I would lay the evidence before Si Denton and have him send for the territorial marshall and the judge. I had no doubt that Thick would also implicate Frey when caught and tried for murdering Edwards.

CHAPTER 11

Edwards proved to be as much trouble dead as he was breathing. I remembered a printed poster on the wall of the jail that offered a reward for the villain, dead or alive. It seemed to me that the cash offered for his capture had not been significant enough for a man to risk his life to obtain it. However, since Edwards was already dead and my pockets were altogether empty, I determined that I would bring in the corpse and trade him for bacon and beans.

The problem was, that antique relic of a horse left me back at Bone's had turned up lame. Not just a mite lame, neither, but full-blown stove-up lame. I turned him out, knowing his instincts would drive him toward lower altitude, pasture, and water.

It was forty-five miles back to Genoa. I now had but one horse with which to haul my grisly freight. This meant I had to walk the entire distance and lead Shad after me. It would be slow going. Such an enterprise would take at least two days at a quick march. After that length of time with Edwards slung over the saddle,

I figured the body would be ripe as old sauerkraut, stiff as a post, and bent into the permanent shape of a horse-shoe. The undertaker would have to stuff him, rear-end-side up, into a rain barrel in order to bury him.

I apologized to Shad as I rolled Edwards up in a length of canvas tent, bound him like a hog, and hefted him across my saddle. Expressing the sincere hope that I could find a shorter route back to Genoa, we set out.

The first several miles of our trek lay over the well-beaten Emigrant Trail back across Border Ruffian Pass. After six hours I came to the place where the famil-iar road branched left through Faith, Charity, and Hope valleys. On my right, the unnamed Indian track taken by the cattle-thieving savages snaked away down a steep canyon. It seemed to me that it might cut a shorter route to the floor of the Carson Valley.

I took the less traveled route, moving at a good clip down the mountain. After an hour, we came to a clear-ing. I rested Shad there for thirty minutes, allowing him to graze where the bones of oxen bleached in the sun. I unloaded Edwards beside a heap of household goods that had been discarded by immigrants years before as they faced the towering mountains. A rusting cookstove kept mournful company beside a mahogany picture frame and a milking stool.

The edge of the clearing was thick with a tangle of wild rosebushes. Were these left behind by some pio-neer? Had they been planted on the grave of a wife or child and then multiplied into a thicket? For a moment I considered scooping out a shallow grave for Edwards in this place, but common sense got the better of me. I resaddled Shad and hefted Edwards onto my horse's back. Gathering rose haw, or seed pods, from the tangle of wild rosebushes at the edge of the field, I popped them into my mouth, then pocketed another handful for the journey. I had learned of this source of nourishment from the Indians, who ate the wild rose haw like candy. They helped to stave off sickness, the Shoshone claimed, and made teeth strong. I had simply developed a taste for them.

From the meadow, we traveled down the narrow path through a succession of clearings much like the first. We entered a dense forest that rose in solemn stillness around me and cast shadows which seemed to me an almost tangible omen of approaching evil.

I told myself the uneasiness I felt was spurred on by the fact that I had none for company save a dead man, but even Shad seemed skittish about something. I began to sing hymns in order to comfort myself, but as the shadows deepened, so did my foreboding.

The sun set early. I had made only little more than half the distance I intended. Still, I pushed on through the forest shadows. The moon rose full and bright in the east, lighting the mountains in a monochrome glow. Now I walked in silence, listening to the creeping night sounds all around me. An owl hooted as we passed below him. The rush of bat wings swept close past my head. From the canyon beyond, brush wolves began to howl with screams that sounded like humans in torment.

I considered all the fragments of the puzzle surrounding Lucky's death—the part that Edwards and Thick had played. It was a picture somewhat like the moonlit landscape surrounding me. Gray and shadowy and full of unseen threats. I now knew more of the who, but still had not the key to why.

There had been nights riding herd when a newborn calf was lost in a thicket. Its mama would bawl and fret until I lit out and brought it back. In such times it came to me that the Lord knew the answer to where that baby was. Only the Lord could help me find it before some mountain lion took it home for supper. I had often found the remains of the calf, but my search had not ended there. I had then gone on to hunt the lion.

The predator who had killed Lucky was still on the loose; now he was stalking me. I felt this as I walked through the deepening shadows that night. I needed help that was beyond my own power, and I called upon the Lord to show me which way to walk next.

The wind rose. Clouds from the northeast passed across the moon and gave the scene an even more weird and somber character.

I said to Shad, "As long as the moon gives us light, we'll get on with it." Then I explained to my horse that if we did not press on, it would likely take three days to get Edwards back to Genoa, off the saddle, and into the barrel. Shad seemed willing to go ahead as long as I did.

The hour was late when the moon finally slipped below the western peaks. Stars frosted the sky above us, but on the ground, utter blackness descended, making further progress impossible.

I unceremoniously dumped Edwards at the base of a tree some distance away. Shad was hobbled with rawhide loops around his forelegs which enabled him to graze on the thin grass. Sensing that a campfire might draw unwanted guests, I made cold camp and fed myself on dry crackers, jerked venison, and wild rose haw.

Sometimes the most confusing, tangled circumstances have the easiest solutions. Unfortunately, it is also true that just when things appear straightforward, they are most likely to get complicated or take an unexpected turn.

Such was the case with my plans.

When I was still traversing Border Ruffian Pass, keeping a sharp lookout for Indian raiders or an ambush by Thick, the real trouble was unfolding down in Genoa.

Thick had ridden hard all night and made good time. And why not? He was mounted on the stolen race horse, Bald Hornet.

He changed mounts at Frey's ranch, so as not to be too conspicuous, then went into town and tied up behind Frey's hotel. He went up the back stair to the second floor and Major Frey's private office, where he burst in.

The Major was none too pleased at the interruption, either, since he had a saloon gal sitting on his lap. He jumped up abruptly, dumping the girl on the floor, where she landed with a squawk. "Get out, Phoebe," he hissed at her. "And close the door."

She got up, rubbing her backside where she had bounced off a spittoon, and left as ordered.

"What is this?" the Major demanded soon as the door was shut. "I told you never to come here! There must not be any connection between us! Now get out, Thick! Come to the ranch tonight, after dark."

"No," Thick disagreed, shaking his ponderous jowls. "You need to hear this, and it won't keep."

Something in the bearlike man's serious tone convinced Frey of urgency. He waved Thick into a chair and reseated himself. "All right, spill it."

"There's another Thornton, Lucky's brother, nosing around."

"Old news." Frey discarded the information with a wave of his hand. He extracted a cigar from a brass-bound walnut case and examined it, leaning toward a copper-and-glass smoking lamp.

"Then hear this: Thornton found Edwards. Caught him in the lean-to."

"What?" the Major said, biting the end off the cigar with more force than strictly necessary. "What did Edwards tell him, and where are they now?"

"I don't know what all Thornton knows. Edwards

swore he said nothing, but I wasn't there when they were alone. I helped Edwards escape . . ."

Frey rose up in his chair and drew a Colt pocket revolver out of the cigar box. "You did what?" he shouted, waving the pistol in one hand and the stub of his cigar in the other. "You idiot! How could you let him get away?"

"Calm down, boss," Thick pleaded, spreading his mittlike palms. "I didn't say he was alive."

The Major subsided, settling back in his leather chair. "Go on."

"I clobbered Thornton over the head, and Edwards and me took off. When we got clean up to Petrified Valley, I killed him."

"And Thornton?" Frey asked eagerly. "Did you finish him too?"

Thick shook his head. "I dunno. He's got an awful hard head. I could hear someone calling for me from the station, so I grabbed Edwards, and we lit out. Even if Thornton follows, he's way behind. Edwards took his horse, and I rode Bald Hornet. The palomino is at your place."

The Major leaned back in his chair, furrows creasing his forehead. Thick waited a respectful time, then carefully ventured, "There's more. Thornton found the bodies of the emigrants. He's spreading the word about the Indian raids."

The Major said nothing, but gradually a smile crept across his face. "It's perfect," he said. "Two birds with

one stone . . . or maybe three? Thick, you are more valuable than I thought. You've done well. Now here's what
I want you to do. Go to Constable Denton. Tell him that
you were on the way here to pass along information
about the wanted man, Edwards, when you found the
bodies of the emigrants. Tell him there needs to be a
posse formed at once, then you lead them. Only don't
take Bald Hornet; leave him in my barn. I'll handle the
rest."

What was it that roused me from deep sleep? The
morning air was bitter cold, as it often is in the high
mountains just before sunrise. I tucked my face deeper
beneath the rough, warm wool of my bedroll and began
to drift off again.

There was a moment between waking and slumber
when the sound of Shad's abrupt snort jerked me back to
consciousness. Right after that I heard the noise of leaves
rustling beneath a shuffling footfall. Sitting bolt upright
in the blue light of predawn, I strained to see who or
what approached my camp.

Shad called and strained against the rawhide hobble
that held him. A dark shape emerged from the thicket of
manzanita and lumbered toward the canvas-wrapped
corpse of Edwards. It was a young bear, a grizzly I reckoned, by the shape of the hump on its back. It had caught
a whiff of Edwards and had come for breakfast.

With a squall, it swiped at the body with its claws, rolling Edwards up against the tree with no more effort than a child tossing a toy.

"Four-legged vulture," I said as the beast tore at the canvas.

Shad screamed and tried to rear. I rushed to grasp his halter and hold him steady against his terror. Tossing his head, he connected hard with my chin and sent me sprawling. I jumped to my feet again and talked softly to calm my horse. Shad fought against the hobbles, lunging and stumbling as he attempted to put some distance between himself and the cub.

Leaving Edwards to the bear, I plunged after Shad. "Whoa up, son," I called gently. "It's just a young'un."

It was no use. Shad had smelled the bear and would not be hindered. I let him go, figuring he could not get far with the hobbles. Better to scare the cub away from Edwards first and then catch up with my horse.

Even a young grizzly in search of food can be deadly when challenged, so I paused long enough to grab the repeater from its scabbard. My thinking was to scare the critter off, rather than taking a chance on wounding it. Grizzlies are notoriously hard to kill. I fired a shot into the air, and the cub let out a long mournful growl. It hesitated a moment, then proceeded to rip at the fabric again.

Fumbling for my tin plate, I banged it against the rifle stock and whooped a few times as I advanced up the slope against the young marauder. Had I known what waited at the head of the trail, I would have turned and run for my life with Shad. I should have abandoned Edwards, who was past caring anyway, but it went against my grain to leave him as a meal for a bear. Anyway, the thought of the reward gave me too much courage.

Any experienced mountain man knows that where there is a young grizzly, there is likely to be an old one close at hand. Owing to the late season, I had assumed this critter had been abandoned and left to make his own way in the wild. That assumption proved to be dead wrong. I was about to meet Mama Grizzly.

Three steps nearer, I gave a Paiute war cry, yelping like a brush wolf. Baby bear gave me a worried glance over his shoulder and retreated from Edwards.

"Git!" I cried bravely, hurling a stone at him. He bawled unhappily and scooted away a few yards.

I was feeling something like David must have felt when he ran the lions away from his herds of sheep. Then suddenly, as the small bear charged along the trail, an enormous black boulder came to life one hundred feet from where I stood. It was not a boulder, but a mountain of Mama Grizzly which reared up on its haunches and fractured the Sierras with the sound of its roar. Upright, she towered a full nine feet. A thousand pounds of fury advanced toward me. Saliva dripped from her bared fangs as she pictured me as the main course in her last supper before hibernation.

All the nearby trees had their bottom-most limbs too

high up to reach. There was no retreating that way, or I would have taken it.

Dropping my dinner plate, I raised the Volcanic to my shoulder and fired at her chest, which was some ways over my head. The shot was received with yet another roar! She brushed at the wound as though it were of no more significance than a fly and continued her advance. Malice flared in her eyes. I backed a step and fired again. The second bullet did not stop her, nor did the third or the fourth.

Levering and firing as I backed up, I knew better than to turn and run. Grizzlies can move down hill like freight trains, like avalanches!

All too soon the hammer fell on an empty chamber. There was no time to reload the tube magazine. You cannot call for time out when facing a half ton of buzz saw. I was a goner. Soon enough the pair of grizzlies would have two carcasses to feast on. The sow slashed at the empty air, dropped to all fours, and moved down the slope, shaking her head from side to side. She was intent on ripping me to shreds.

I stumbled backwards, falling over my saddle. The rifle flew from my hands. I scrambled to open my saddlebag and groped for Edwards's pocket revolver. Thirty-one caliber was not much more than a peashooter against a beast with the size of an ox and the disposition of an alligator, but it was not in my nature to go down without a fight.

Since the bear was rumbling toward me like a wave about to dash a rowboat against a reef, I did the only thing I could think of to gain time: I started backing uphill as fast as I could, praying that the manzanita and chaparral underfoot would not trip me and become my final resting place.

The nearsighted silvertip got distracted for a moment by the saddle, which she almost knocked into the next county. Then Edwards received another blow that would have killed him had he not already been defunct. Then Mama Grizzly caught my scent again, and her head swung back toward me.

Grizzlies are slower-moving uphill than down, and the change in her onslaught made her rear up again to get her bearings. It may also have been that my earlier shots were finally having an effect. When she opened her mouth to let out another bellow, I put a shot between her gaping jaws.

The bullet struck her in the back of the throat, but even before I knew this, I thumbed back the hammer and fired two more rounds in the same spot. The sow toppled over backward like a falling tree, and the cub bolted for the tall timber.

I set about retrieving the remains of my gear and catching Shad, whose timely alert had once more spared my life. It took me some time to piece together shreds of canvas to again load Edwards for travel.

CHAPTER 12

Si Denton was not slack about gathering a posse when he heard Thick's description of slaughtered emigrants stuck full of Paiute arrows. Deputy Hawkins rounded up Manny Penrod, Lute Olds, Curtis Raycraft, and others and assembled them in front of the courthouse. Even Bernard King showed up.

"Men," Constable Denton said. "These murders are the worst threat to the safety of this region in ten years. We have had a season of stampeded stock and wounded drovers, but now there's been killings, and the raids must stop. Now, who'll ride with me?"

"We all will!" Raycraft asserted. "And we won't waste time about it either! Let's ride straight to Winnemucca's camp and wipe them out!"

Growls of agreement were accompanied by the brandishing of weapons. "Now that's exactly what I will not have," Si ordered sternly. "We are after the braves who killed the two men and no others! Is that clear? I am out to bring the guilty to justice and to prevent a war, not

start one. Anyone who doesn't see it my way will not be
coming along, if I end up going by myself!"

There was a great deal of grumbling at this declaration. "Shoot," Paul Hawkins murmured on the front
porch next to Si, "all we want to do is make good
Indians out of them."

Si rounded on him fiercely. "That'll be all of that
from you, too, Paul! Either back my play, or hand over
your star!" The deputy ducked his head and said nothing
further, but Si was not done lecturing the others. "This
isn't about vengeance," he insisted, "it's about justice.
That's the difference between law and mob rule! Now I
say again, if you don't agree, I don't want you."

The grousing did not completely subside, but a dozen
riders were mounted up and ready to head out in less
time than it takes to spit. Thick led the troop up into the
Sierras, past Waterfords Station, and down the road into
Hope Valley.

The trail narrowed in a rocky gorge to where they
had to walk their horses and single file at that. Thick was
riding point, followed by Hawkins on a roan, and then
Si Denton on his big, easily recognizable paint named
Cimarron.

Si, old Indian fighter that he was, glanced up at the
walls of the ravine towering over both sides of the track.
It was a perfect spot for an ambush. But such an attack
was unlikely, given the strength of the posse and their
obvious firepower. Any Paiutes that were this close to the
Carson Valley would undoubtedly have gotten wind of

the pursuit and fled. Si did not expect to locate the killers until tracking them back to their encampment, and that could take days.

A flash of tawny hide appeared briefly between the gnarled trunks of a pair of wind-twisted bristle-cone pines. "Cougar?" Paul Hawkins guessed, bending around in his saddle to ask Si if he had also seen the animal.

Hawkins saw Si Denton open his mouth to reply, but the response was never completed. The boom of a big-bore rifle, like a Sharps or a Springfield, split the afternoon's tranquillity.

As if Si had been riding full tilt and reached the end of a tether, he snapped backward off the paint horse and flew through the air. In midflight, Hawkins saw the constable's chest bloom with a bright red flower. Cimarron spooked and galloped forward, jostling Hawkins's horse as it tried to get by in the confined space. Both mounts reared and plunged while Hawkins drew his pistol and scanned the ledges. Behind him Lute Olds fired both barrels of his shotgun into the canyon wall. Bernard King drew his pocket revolver and fired it straight up into the air.

"Ride!" Thick yelled back. "It's death to stay in here!" and the big man clapped the spurs to his mount and galloped ahead.

No more shots came. Though the riders had been as much in a box trap as rats caught pilfering grain, they rode forward unchallenged. "There he goes," Thick shouted, pointing ahead.

"Olds," Hawkins ordered. "You and Penrod take care of Si. The rest of you, follow me!"

The chase led up out of the canyon along a narrow ledge that opened out on top of the mesa. The sniper was too far away for his features to be recognizable, but the honey-colored palomino was easy to follow. Also, it was plain that this was no Indian.

At first the assassin appeared headed for Border Ruffian Pass. He skirted Little Blue Lake, but that was where Hawkins and the other pursuers made a mistake. Instead of riding up both sides of the small body of water, they followed the palomino along the west shore. When the fugitive reached the head of the pool, he doubled back, turning the corner so that the lake lay between him and the posse. Then the rider on the tawny horse charged up the top of the ridge and took off northward.

Hawkins urged his horse to its greatest effort, and for a period of some minutes, he succeeded in gaining on the escaping sharpshooter. Though all the others in the pursuit were winded, blown, and dropping back, Hawkins was gaining.

In his anger and frustration, he drew his Colt again, even though he knew it was long odds against hitting anything at the two-hundred-yards distance that separated the two horses. Hawkins fired, thumbed back the hammer, fired again, and was rewarded with seeing the palomino horse stumble.

Hawkins gave a shout of triumph, but his cry of success died in his throat. It had only been a loose rock, and not a wound, that made the yellow racer falter. The palomino put on a sudden burst of speed and spurted ahead, pulling away and foiling any additional shots by darting into the trees.

The deputy spurred and kicked, but his roan was spent. In a matter of a few minutes more, the yellow horse and the shooter were completely out of sight, still heading north, back toward the Carson Valley.

Hawkins reined up and waited for Thick and the others to join him. He put Thick on the track of the sniper while he himself retraced his path toward the canyon where the constable had been shot.

He caught up with Penrod and Olds not far from the place of the attack. They were pulling Si on a willow-frame travois. "Why aren't you further along?" Hawkins demanded. "Si's hurt bad; why don't you bustle?" Even as he asked the question Hawkins knew the reason: It was too late for Si Denton, and no amount of rushing would make a difference now.

"What about the killer?" Penrod wanted to know. "Did you get him?"

Hawkins shook his head grimly. "No," he reported. "But if we catch up with him before he has a chance to change mounts, we'll know him beyond any doubt. And even if he trades off that palomino, he'll leave a trail a mile wide."

It took me some time to get ready to leave the scene of the combat with the bears, but my legs were still trembling. They say that some folks feel weak in the knees when facing danger, but with me, I have always found that the shakes come afterward. Perhaps if I had better sense, I would know enough to be frightened beforehand.

Shad snorted so at the aroma of dead grizzly that I had to lead him off a ways before he would let me saddle him. Even then he whuffed and stamped at the smell of the bears on the canvas shroud. It was just as well that I would be walking and leading because he seemed uncommonly fractious.

A half mile down the trail toward the valley of the Carson, Shad suddenly threw up his head and whinnied in that deep-voiced way of his that sounds almost like an elk bugling. I hunted up the Volcanic double-quick. It was not likely that another bear would be so close to the territory patrolled by the sow and her cub, but given my recent escape I would take no chances.

Whatever was disturbing Shad lay across the trail just ahead, because he shied and began to prance sideways. The canyon was too narrow to go around whatever it was, and we had come too far to retrace our steps. I tied Shad to a tree and went forward to reconnoiter.

The breeze that swirled up from the valley brought me the answer. There was the smell of death on the wind; the metallic scent of old blood and decay.

On this occasion I marked the location of a handy-limbed climbing tree before proceeding further, but my caution was unfounded. All that disturbed the morning was the savaged remains of a steer. The bears had plainly been at the carrion and had scattered bones and hide about a small clearing in which was set a crude corral. Someone had used a small box canyon as a temporary pen for cow critters by driving them into the stone-walled draw and then blocking the entrance with a brush arbor.

From the tracks I guessed that the Paiutes had driven their stolen property to this spot. While holding the herd here, they had butchered one of the steers to feed their band. Mama grizzly had come upon the offal after the Indians and their plundered stock had gone on.

All this information was told me by the ground—by the tracks of moccasins, horses, cattle, and bears. But something was wrong, disturbing the satisfaction of my conclusion. It was not a worry or a threat exactly, at least not a present danger. The nagging concern was more a notion that I was missing something important.

Idly kicking at a palm-sized piece of dark red hide, I reflected how the bears had left virtually nothing of use to their survival. As the bit of cowhide flipped up in the air, I found myself staring at the print of a booted foot. Paiutes did not often wear boots in those days. Could the track be my own, I wondered? A quick comparison showed the step to be too small to be me. Of course, it could have been stolen from a settler. Maybe some brave had taken a fancy to white men's footgear.

Then the full truth struck me with a rush, and I saw clearly what had been right in front of me all along. Indians, like bears, waste nothing. Even if they had felt secure enough in this canyon to kill and cook a beef, they would have packed out the hide. No Indian, unless in a terrible hurry, would butcher a steer and leave the hide for scavengers. Leather was clothing and shelter and trade goods—far too valuable to be left behind.

That was the answer, plain as the nose on Rough Elliott's face. The raids on cattle had not been the work of Indians but of whites masquerading as Indians. The reason the one dead man had bled so on his front but not from the arrow in his back was because the arrow had been plunged in after his death. A fistful of Paiute arrows and the finger of accusation pointed square at the Indians. The rustlers had even worn moccasins for the attack to hide their identities, but down here in the corral, one had gotten careless.

Now I felt like I knew it all. This was the secret my brother Lucky had held over the Major; this was the information that had gotten him killed. Frey and his gang had been driving off the herds of the emigrant parties, and somehow Lucky had tumbled to that fact.

Major Frey had then manufactured a way of seeing that Lucky could not tell anyone, ever.

Days and nights at the sawmill were mighty peaceful after I left. Hard labor and the expectation of the return of King and Elliott kept the restless mind of Kit entertained for a short time. When the dam was completed and it became apparent that there was nothing to protect Maria and the children against, Kit became rapidly bored.

As I was struggling to get Edwards back to Genoa and safely deposited with the undertaker, Kit was playing mumblety-peg with George and losing.

Kit said to George as they sat on the top step and tossed the knife at the target, "I reckon you surely do regret that you cannot go to school with the other boys and girls."

"Not so much." George hit the circle dead center. "You're almost as much fun."

Kit plucked the blade from the ground and sat back. He took aim, threw, and missed. "What about girls?" he asked George.

"What about them?"

"Aren't you old enough to be noticing females?"

"Sure. Notice what?"

"Aren't there some pretty ones at school in Genoa?"

George scratched his pomaded head with one finger

and peered up at the sky as if he could not recollect seeing any. He replied with a quick negative shake of his head. "All the ones my age are taller than me. The younger ones are missing teeth. They all hate boys, and we hate them."

"That makes you fortunate." Kit threw and lost to George again. "You seen Angie Frey?"

"Yeah. Major Frey's niece. Works at the cafe."

"Think she's pretty?"

"I never thought about it," George answered truthfully.

"I can't stop thinking about it. Here I am at the sawmill. Stuck here. Day after day. I would go down to Genoa and pay her a call if it wasn't for that mule. I won't go riding into Genoa on that Army jackass."

"Uncle John said you ought to stay here all the same."

Kit's eyes narrowed at the mention of my name. "John just didn't want me going anywhere at all. He just wants me to stay here and . . ."

"Stay out of trouble," George finished.

Kit sighed. "I wouldn't go pay Angie a call riding on that old mule anyway. I would be a laughingstock."

The two sat in silence, staring at the broken flume. Then George said, "My dad thought a lady at Frey's saloon was pretty. Miss Nell. She is a . . . a harlot."

Kit gawked at him. "Who told you that?"

"Billy Teckler at school. What is a harlot?"

"Never you mind."

George cocked his head sideways. "Was he lying?"

"Never you mind," Kit tried to dodge the subject.

"Must be something awful if you won't tell me. I seen it in the Bible. In daily devotions Mother won't so much as read the word out loud, so I sneaked back and looked, but it don't explain nothing."

George rambled on awhile about different harlots in the Good Book, and the talk of it made Kit nervous. After all, Maria had made Kit swear he would not talk with George about all the wrong that Lucky had done.

"Well," Kit said as he got up. "I guess I'm going to ride up to the ridge and have a look."

"What for?" George asked.

"In case someone is coming," Kit answered him gruffly.

George grinned. "You just want to go away and think about Angie someplace where I won't see you mooning."

George was partly right, but Kit did not let the boy know it. He snatched up the repeater, saddled the mule, and headed for the ridge where he could sit and look down over the valley and think about Angie Frey without the boy asking anymore questions about Lucky and the harlot named Miss Nell.

An autumn haze concealed the valley floor below him, but Kit could not get it out of his mind that Angie was down below wishing for him to come pay a call. He closed his eyes and imagined her face. He pictured her serving the rowdy types who came into town to eat at

Frey's. This made his blood boil. It came to him that he ought to be down there in Genoa protecting her from the likes of King instead of sitting up here waiting for King to arrive.

Kit cursed the mule he was riding. He squinted his eyes and, using the mule's ears like a gun sight, he peered away off down Sawmill Road.

It was then that he first noticed something moving at a fast jog up toward the sawmill. First he thought it was a deer. Then, as the animal emerged from the haze, Kit made out that the critter was a horse—a riderless palomino.

How could he know that this was the very animal that figured so prominently in a murder? Kit was a hot-blooded fool, but I cannot blame him for his actions in this matter. The prospect of disaster and total ruin multiplied for us from the moment Kit laid eyes on Bald Hornet, then set out to catch him and ride him into Genoa.

Kit had heard of Bald Hornet. The horse was a legend in gold country. Kit knew, like every other man on both sides of the Sierras, that the racehorse had been stolen from its rightful owner in Placerville and used in a number of escapes from the law.

The sensible thing for Kit to do would have been to get up on his own mule and lead that stolen horse west over the tollroad that led to Placerville. Once there, he could have returned the animal and maybe even collected a reward. But Kit was not sensible. He was smitten to imbecility by Angie Frey. She just happened to be one hundred and eighty degrees in the opposite direction from where Bald Hornet belonged. For this reason alone, Kit planned to ride Bald Hornet eastward to Genoa.

Kit, with help from George, uncovered an old bronc saddle in the tackroom. Too prideful to ride into town on his mule, Kit threw the saddle onto the back of Bald Hornet instead. It did not occur to him that a man caught riding a stolen horse might well be accused of being the thief. Many an innocent man had got his neck stretched from the stout limb of an oak tree for being intercepted with another man's horse or herding another man's steer. Hang first, ask questions later had become the policy when dealing with missing livestock.

No doubt it was Kit's intent to turn the stolen animal over to Si Denton after he visited his lady love. He ponied the mule along behind so he would have a mount to ride back up to the sawmill after dark. But it was foolhardy for him to ride the stolen horse.

He did not meet a soul on the way to Genoa. Outside of town he tied his mule to a tree lest Angie see it. Kit rode the last half mile into Genoa on Bald Hornet, arriving at the rear entrance of Frey's establishment. Leaving the horse at the hitching rail among a half dozen other mounts, Kit went in under the pretext that he wanted a meal.

Angie was clearing tables in the restaurant, which was empty after the noon seating. In the adjacent saloon, the remnant of the posse were drowning their misery at the death of Si Denton. Frey and Rough Elliott were at the center of the group. Frey had provided drinks on the house, and the rage of the men seemed to increase as more whiskey was consumed.

Kit, knowing nothing of these terrible events, entered the cafe with a grin on his face. He doffed his hat when Angie Frey looked up at him, and he stammered that he wished a pitcher of cow's milk and a bowl of cornbread.

Angie, blushing at the sight of him, seated Kit at the table in the back corner of the room. "There is also one fine piece of roast beef left in the warmer," she said. "The posse fairly cleaned us out of every other morsel."

"Posse?" Kit asked.

"You haven't heard?" Angie fetched the milk and brought cornbread in a bowl. Pouring the milk over the cornbread, she told Kit the news about the ambush and murder of Si Denton. What she failed to mention was the fact that the murderer had been seen making his escape on a palomino horse thought to be Bald Hornet. If only Kit had known that one small piece of information, everything might have turned out differently for him.

"Si Denton killed?" This was a blow to Kit. Si had been kind while Kit had been in jail. Kit became attached to the constable, as a man will do when kept in such close quarters for three months.

"Those fellows in there with my uncle?" Angie lowered her voice. "They say when they catch up with who did it . . ."

She did not finish the sentiment. Paul Hawkins, his badge gleaming on his vest and fury in his eye, burst through the front door. He carried a loaded double-barreled shotgun, which he cradled in his arms.

Kit had just taken a bite of cornbread. He raised his hand to greet Hawkins.

Hawkins asked, "You ride into town on that yeller horse, Kit Thornton?"

"Sorry to hear the news about Si."

"Lawrence Frey says he seen you ride into town on that yeller horse tied out back."

"I reckon that was me."

"Bald Hornet, ain't it?" The buzz of angry conversation hushed in the saloon as Paul Hawkins stepped nearer toward Kit.

"I intended to bring him round to Si after I ate . . ." Kit faltered when he saw the look of pure hatred that filled Hawkins's face.

Hawkins spoke in a low, menacing voice. "Move away from the table, Miss Angie. There's a rattlesnake coiled up behind you, and I intend to see it don't strike nobody else."

Angie grew pale. She looked down at Kit, then

backed away. Hawkins swung the barrel of the shotgun around and pointed it full at Kit's head.

The spoon dropped from Kit's hand. "What . . . what . . . is this?"

Hawkins glared at him. "We all seen Bald Hornet runnin' full gallop after Si was killed."

From the saloon an angry voice repeated that Kit Thornton had ridden Bald Hornet into town. Other voices joined in an angry chorus. A crowd of enraged faces appeared at the doorway.

Kit spread his hands in a gesture of innocence. "I only just found the horse wandering loose on Sawmill Road, Hawkins! I swear I . . . I was bringing the horse back here to . . ."

"Save it! Hands over your head!"

"I tell you I was only . . ."

"Hands up, I said! You are under arrest for the murder of Si Denton, and I, for one, intend to be there when you hang!"

CHAPTER 13

Without any warning about what had happened during my absence, Shad and I, together with the aging corpse, arrived back in Genoa. I will admit that we were a spectacle as we headed up Main Street toward the courthouse. I spared a glance for Frey's place, but I fended off the temptation to confront him at once with his crimes. Cornering something low-down and sneaky like a badger is liable to have unpleasant consequences. My plan was to lay my evidence, so to speak, directly before Si Denton, tell him all I knew, and then let the law take its course.

The gaping eyes and wagging tongues that followed my progress I attributed to the obvious. It never occurred to me that the whispers and the pointing had more to do with me than with Edwards.

Shad was standing patiently at the rail, and I was untying the rawhide thongs with which the corpse was bound to the saddle. "Hey, sonny," I called to a dirty-faced street rat loafing nearby. "Get Constable

Denton. Tell him John Thornton wants to see him muy pronto."

Instead of running into the courthouse like I figured, this kid stared till I thought his eyes would pop. Then a female, his mama I reckoned, dashed out of a dry goods store across the street. She grabbed that youngster by his shoulder, whirled him around, and marched him straight off. But the strangest thing of all was the look she gave me—like I was the worst desperado to hit those parts since Joaquin Murietta. I mean, she looked scared.

While I was still undoing the bands, the scene with the kid just about replayed itself. A hand laid rough on my shoulder, and I was jerked around sharp. That is where the similarity ended, because Paul Hawkins's fist landed right on the point of my jaw.

I jostled Shad, who jumped sideways, and the canvas containing Edwards shucked his remains right out in the middle of the street whilst I sprawled on the ground beside it. "What in blazes did you do that for?" I demanded. I made a move to jump up, when I suddenly saw I was nose-to-nose with a forty-four.

"Get up slow and easy," Hawkins ordered. "Keep your hands where I can see 'em all the time, or you won't live to figure out what you did wrong." Hawkins jerked my rifle out of the scabbard.

"What is all this?" I said, all the while taking him at his word and rising slowly to my feet. Now my chin hurt, and the back of my head started aching all over again.

"I'll say this for you, Thornton," Hawkins said, waving me toward the courthouse with his pistol. "You've got some kind of sand to come waltzin' in here."

"What nonsense is this?" I wanted to know. "This hunk of earth is Edwards," I said, touching the body with the toe of my boot, "but I didn't kill him. I followed him from Bone's, but somebody else shot him and left him for dead. Get Si, and I'll explain everything."

Hawkins swung his pistol barrel toward my head like he was going to clock me with it. I ducked, and he stopped just short of taking out my teeth. "You are a cold character," he concluded, much to my confusion, "but it don't matter none. I figure you're a party to the killing, and you'll hang same as Kit."

"Kit?" I said, stunned into using real short words. "What now?"

"It won't do you any good to pretend you don't know," Hawkins said. "We caught Kit dead to rights after he bushwhacked Si. I just didn't think it would be so easy to take you."

There are times when a man can do a heap of thinking in a mighty brief spell of time, and right then was one of those times. It came to me like a flash of lightning that Kit was in terrible danger. If Si was really dead, what if Paul Hawkins was part of the vigilantes? It would mean that Kit, and me, too, for that matter, could be blamed and hanged before anyone gave it a second thought.

If Kit was to be saved, there was no other course but for me to remain free. As I say, all this stampeded through my mind in less time than it takes to tell.

Hawkins had unknowingly done me a favor by laying hold of my repeater the way he had. Every man alive has one hand that works better than the other, and encumbering the one mitt always seems to interfere with both.

As we started up the plank steps of the courthouse, I knew in that instant what I was going to do. I let Hawkins crowd me a bit, getting closer back of me. As I stepped up with my right foot and the weight came off my left leg, I drew it back sharp and gave a low kick that hit him on the right knee. At the same second, I pivoted my body around and clamped both my hands around his right wrist—the hand holding the pistol. With his body being knocked one direction and me pulling the other, I almost broke his hold on the gun.

The Colt exploded with a roar, the slug tearing a half-inch-deep furrow in the oak planks of the county treasurer's floor after busting out his window. Folks dove for cover, but there was really no more danger to them; there was no way I was going to let him cock the hammer back for another shot.

Exactly as I figured, Hawkins knew that I would win the battle for the pistol if we continued my two hands against his one. He did the only thing he could do, which was let go of my rifle. He flung the lever action as hard as he could. The Volcanic slithered across the ground like a thing alive and, worse luck, went under the courthouse steps, out of reach.

Shad, who had never been hard-tied, jerked away from the rail and backed up a few steps as if giving us room to wrestle. The gunshot had sent all the onlookers off the street, so our only company in the struggle was the body of Edwards, which was mostly clothespin shaped.

Now we were more evenly matched, with Hawkins's Colt stuck between us both. I could hear voices shouting all up and down Main Street and knew that my time was fast running out.

Hawkins and I rolled over in the dirt of the courthouse yard. We were both head-butting and kicking our knees up, but neither of us was willing to give up a grip on the pistol to throw a punch.

Then I spotted the stone mounting step a few feet away and knew what I had to do. Rolling furiously, I got up a good bit of speed across the ground. Keeping to a straight course in such a melee was like lassoing a grizzly: It's almost impossible and you only get one chance to do it right. By sheer providence, I completed the third rotation when our movement was stopped abruptly by the contact between Hawkins's head and the granite block.

His eyes crossed and his grip on the Colt slackened. In that moment I wrenched the pistol free, jumped up from across him, and bolted for Shad. The bay skittered away from me, trailing the reins, and I ran alongside, reaching up for the horn.

It is surely true that to have one hand encumbered when you need both for a piece of business means no good will result. I planted both feet and sprang up for the saddle in a running mount, using Shad's momentum to propel me into the seat. But I lost my hold on the revolver even as I got aboard Shad's back. The last I saw of the weapon, it was flying through the air, heading toward Lute Olds's feed lot.

Even weaponless, I counted myself successful as Shad sprinted out of town. I had no thought for the moment other than escape; I would fill in the details later. But I had reckoned without Lawrence Frey, who despite his youth, showed more presence of mind than all the grown men of Genoa.

Lawrence had been approaching Main Street from the north when he heard the shot and saw the struggle going on in front of the courthouse. Instead of riding into a shooting war, he tossed a loop of his riata around a branch of the giant water oak that marked the northern boundary of town. Then he rode across the highway and dismounted.

Taking a turn of the hemp rope around a fence post, he dropped the slack in the dirt and waited. When Shad and I thundered toward freedom, Lawrence yanked the line taut, blocking the road.

Shad tucked his head when he saw the barrier rise up in front of him, but I had used up all my quick thinking

for the day: I forgot to duck. The trap set by Lawrence
Frey clotheslined me, and I have counted myself fortunate ever since that it did not break my neck.

As it was, the line caught me across the midsection
and cleaned me out of the saddle while my horse ran on
without me. I landed flat on my back. I was not knocked
out, though winded a mite. Aside from disappointment
at not making good my escape, my first thought was how
tired I was of being beat up and abused by men, grizzly
bears, and hard, hard ground.

When Hawkins marched me up the courthouse steps
the second time, he did so from behind the triggers of a
double-barreled scattergun. He stayed a respectful distance behind me, too, ordering me to march on ahead or
he would blow me in half. I obliged him because I was
feeling pretty used up by then, and for another reason as
well: I believed him.

He stuck me into the same iron cage with Kit, who, I
must say, was not pleased to see me, at least not under
those circumstances. He looked some the worse for wear
too. His eyes were puffed up and the color of ripe plums,
and his lips were split. Hawkins slammed the door on the
two of us and left us to get reacquainted.

Between holding my ribs and rubbing my head and
jaw, I managed to ask Kit for his story. He told me about
the horse and his capture and what he had heard about

Si Denton's murder. It seems that Bernard King had been real pleased to share the word that the whole valley was up in arms that Si had been ambushed and that hanging was the certain outcome.

I brought my brother up-to-date on my whereabouts and what I now knew to be true about Major Frey and company. "Much good it may do us," I said, "until we get an impartial hearing."

"We don't need a hearing," Kit announced. "I ain't staying to get lynched." He peered out through the grate on the door to see if anyone was about, then dropped to one knee. From his boot top he pulled a knife. "We'll grab whoever brings our supper and cut their throat if they don't get out of our way."

"That's real fine," I said in an offhanded way, leaning forward as if to see the blade. Then I lunged at him, caught the knife handle in both fists, and cracked his wrist down on my knee. Kit squalled and dropped the weapon, which I retrieved and thrust into my own boot.

"Yow!" he complained, shaking the injured arm. "What'd you do that for?"

"Do you want to give them any more reason to shoot or hang us?" I demanded. "Are you trying to prove us guilty? We need a lawman or a judge, not a hostage. You stay cool, and we'll beat this thing yet."

Kit retreated to the corner of the cell, putting us all of ten feet apart. Once there, he sank down to sulk.

Later, when we saw who it was brought our supper, I wondered if Kit recalled what he had said. I doubted it, because when the tap on the door came and Paul Hawkins demanded to know the caller's identity, it was Angie Frey's voice that answered.

Kit sat up and brushed his hand through his hair when he heard her. I swear he was thinking of how to make himself presentable when he was in the hoosegow facing a murder charge! Such is youth.

The door swung open, revealing Hawkins armed as before with the shotgun. When Angie was admitted to the cell, she was carrying a pan whose fragrance announced its contents to be fresh-baked cornbread. In her other hand she carried a clay jug of milk. "You didn't get to eat your cornbread," she said, then she stopped at the sight of Kit's ravaged face. Stepping up close despite Hawkins's warning to keep clear, she stretched out her slender hand and tenderly touched Kit's battered eyes. If he had been butter, he would have turned into a little yellow puddle on the floor.

"Now, Miss Angie," Hawkins scolded. "Your uncle wouldn't like you . . ."

She rounded on him sudden, and there was flame in her countenance. "Did you do this, Paul Hawkins, or did you just let it happen?" she demanded.

Hawkins bristled right back. "Si Denton was shot from ambush, and . . ."

"And you've already decided who did it!"

"Miss Frey," I said softly. "Would you like to help us?"

Before Hawkins could voice a word of protest, Angie stared him into silence. "Certainly," she said. "How?"

"Send for Snowshoe Thompson. He'll know who to bring here that will listen to our side. Then please fetch Maria. She will testify that Kit stole no horse."

"I'll get Snowshoe myself," Angie vowed, "and Maria."

"Your uncle won't . . ." Hawkins tried again.

"Don't you dare say one word to my uncle!" Angie flared. "I am of age and able to make up my own mind!"

With that she marched out, leaving Hawkins dumbfounded, Kit starry-eyed, and me hopeful.

My state of mind did not stay positive for long. Before the sun had dropped behind Monument Peak, the loud-mouthed soaks, brimful of tanglefoot, gathered on the corner opposite the jail. We could not see them, but their boozy voices carried clear to our cell at the back of the building.

"Hang 'em, I say," demanded the growling voice of Rough Elliott. A chorus of agreement responded to his suggestion.

"That's right!"

"String 'em up and be done with it!"

"Stretch their necks 'til their eyes pop for what they did to old Si!"

"The Thornton gang should have been run out of these parts long ago!"

I knew that there was not enough liquor in them yet to make them challenge Hawkins and a double load of buckshot. But he was only one man . . . and what if he stepped aside and let them come?

CHAPTER 14

It seemed right that Snowshoe Thompson lived at the head of Hope Valley because he was our only hope. It had come to me clearly that the fate of Kit and me would be the same as Lucky unless we had someone to speak up for us.

In all the Sierras there was no one man as well-trusted and liked as Snowshoe Thompson. His vocation was delivering the mail to the remote mining camps tucked away in the Sierras. It was his avocation to deliver the souls of men from despair by sharing the hope of the Gospel wherever he went.

In 1853 I had seen him disperse an angry lynch mob on the rampage in the early days of Hangtown by preaching on the gallows steps from midnight until dawn. The three men he had saved were proved to be innocent later on. Once, in Downieville, I had watched him talk sense to a drunken young miner in a saloon who proposed to end his own life by blowing his head off with a scattergun. As Snowshoe counseled the desperate fellow, he leaned so close that the blast would have killed him as well. Snowshoe was a man with a keen sense of justice and no fear whatsoever of death. This enabled him, in the midst of terrible danger, to do the right thing when weaker men stayed out of the line of fire.

Kit and I needed just such a man as this to stand in the gap for us. I knew that if Snowshoe Thompson were able, he would come to our aid in Genoa. If Angie Frey did not find him in time, then he would be the only one to pray over our graves.

Angie, heedless of the disapproval of the Genoa townsfolk, whipped the team up smartly and raced the buckboard through the gathering gloom to Snowshoe's log cabin.

The horses were lathered and spent by the time she turned onto the property. They pulled up short at the door as Snowshoe Thompson stepped out of his house. Before she opened her mouth to speak he figured that someone was bad off.

He reached out to help Angie from the wagon and said in his singsong voice, "Velcome, young lady. Dese here horses is nearly kilt. Nobody drive horses that vey 'less somebody dying and need help."

She collapsed into his arms and managed to gasp out the story of our predicament as Snowshoe calmly looked after the animals, leading them to his barn.

Angie followed after him, talking all the while and finishing with these words, "John Thornton says if you can't help him and Kit tonight, then they will be hanged before morning."

He turned from the hay rack, and a look of understanding filled his eyes. "Yon Thornton is right, for sure. I better git."

With the long, swift strides of a man who routinely covered hundreds of miles of snowy terrain with slender planks strapped to his feet, Snowshoe hurried back to the cabin, where a kettle of stew simmered over the fire. He jerked his thumb at the tin plate waiting on the table. "Eat someting, Miss. Sleep a vile. Come morning, you git up to de sawmill and stay dere with Vidow Thornton and her orphan babies till your horses get rested, den get her to Genoa fast as you can. I'm going to Genoa now." With that pronouncement, he threw another log on the fire, put on his mackinaw, and gathered his Bible, which was open on the table. At the door he remarked quietly over his shoulder, "Ain't no accident you find me here. I vas supposed to be long gone to Placerville, only two days ago I'm prayin', and I git a feeling I'm supposed to stay here and vait."

"But what can I do tonight?"

"You know how to pray, young voman?"

Angie nodded.

He said, "Den you pray I ain't vaited too long."

It was a sleepless night for me, expecting at any moment to be dragged from the cell and hanged from a limb of the same water oak that had arrested my escape. I don't believe that Kit slept a wink, either, despite the fact that we were both beat to thunder.

Earlier than I ever thought possible, I heard Snowshoe Thompson's particular accent and believed again that we might escape with our lives. It was just after midnight when a new ruckus competed with the drunken, angry harangue going on outside.

"You bet you gonna let me in to see dem," Snowshoe argued. "I don't care vat you tink he did. Yon Thornton is a friend of mine, and I vant to speak with him!" The cell door creaked open and Snowshoe was permitted to enter.

The bearded beanpole of a man was the most beautiful sight yet to my blurry eyes. "Thanks for coming, Snowshoe," I said warmly. Then I explained why we were being held and what I knew was behind it all.

Snowshoe had no liking for Major Frey, and he was incensed that we had been arrested on such a flimsy pretext. "But Yon," he warned. "To stay here vhile I go fetch Justice Van Sickle or the marshall is not so good. There is armed men at the hangin' tree. Rough Elliott is bellowin' to everybody who comes how dey don't vant the Thornton gang to break in and set you loose."

I snorted. "The Thornton gang, eh?"

"Dere is no cause of laughin', Yon," Snowshoe said seriously. "If dey play like dere's a gang, dey could also play at shooting you to keep you from escaping, you betcha. And de talk is to hang you now and not vait."

He was right. Stone and steel could not keep a determined mob from dragging us out to meet our doom if such was determined beforehand. "Hawkins," I called to the deputy. "What do you mean to do to keep us from getting lynched?"

Hawkins came to the grate with a sneer on his face. "I sent for the marshall already," he said. "You'll get a fair trial before we hang you. It won't take more'n a couple days."

"Days, he says!" clamored Snowshoe. "You tink dat mob is gonna vait for days? If dey know dat you sent for the marshall, you haf already signed de death varrants for dese two men."

Hawkins did look surprised at the vehemence of the normally peaceful letter carrier. "I told Major Frey to quit setting up free drinks till after the marshall got here," Hawkins protested.

Snowshoe spat angrily, "You told de biggest volf to keep de udder volfs under control? You gotta do better dan dat, Paul Hawkins! Si Denton vouldn't let no mob kill his prisoners, nor see 'em lynched, nor turn over his job to no snake like de Major! Vat you do vhen you gotta sleep, hah?"

I wisely kept my mouth shut and motioned for Kit to do the same. Snowshoe was arguing all the identical points that were in my mind, and Hawkins was listening.

"But what else can I do?" Hawkins demanded.

"Get dem out of here! Take men you trust and get

'em over de mountain to Placerville! And don't vait, do it tonight!"

"But how?" Hawkins mused. "You saw for yourself the mob that's already out there. If we get caught there'll be shooting for sure."

I spoke up for the first time. "What we need is a diversion."

There was a period of silent thought while we all turned this over in our minds, and then Snowshoe said, "Yah. It vill vork. I am this diversion."

"Not good, Snowshoe," I argued. "Even if we get clear away, they'll know who to blame."

Snowshoe shrugged as if the matter was of complete indifference to him. "All of dem is in dere cups tonight. Tomorrow, vhen their heads is aching, dey forget it all already."

"What do you say, Hawkins?" I asked.

The deputy nodded grimly. "If we don't go, I'll end up having to shoot some of the crowd, and I don't want to do that to protect the likes of murderers like you. We'll go."

I did not much like his reasoning, but I was not about to dispute the conclusion.

Thirty minutes later three mounts were tied up in the brush in back of the courthouse. Hawkins bound our hands together with leather thongs, but he left our feet unshackled. I suppose he thought he was giving us a chance to make it if we had to run for it.

Above Rough Elliott's gravelly voice came a new sound. A higher-pitched, piercing speech penetrated the air. "You men stop and tink vat you are about! Do you vant innocent blood on your hands?"

Snowshoe's argument may not have been convincing to the alcohol-addled brains itching for a hanging, but more to the point, it was something different and therefore attention-getting. Snowshoe took up his lecture on the stump of a tree even further out of town to the north, drawing the crowd away from the jail.

To give Hawkins his due, he elected not to trust anyone else with the secret move. That did not mean that he was any more friendly toward us though. "This coach gun is loaded with double-ought," he said, "and buckshot means buryin'. Dark or not, don't try anything funny, or they'll pick up your brains over in Sacramento."

With that he poked his head out the rear door of the jail and looked around. Then he opened the cell and motioned with the shotgun for us to precede him out into the brush. He did not need to tell us to keep perfectly quiet, and I had already warned Kit not to attempt an escape. Even if we somehow avoided being blown to kingdom come, a single shot would bring the mob howling down on us.

We made it across an open space of gravel without incident, but when we entered a draw on the far side Kit stumbled over a tree root. He caught himself from falling with a quick step to the side, but landed squarely on a branch that cracked loudly in the frosty air.

The three of us froze low in the shadows to see if a cry of pursuit was raised, but all we heard was, "Vhen you stand before de Great Judge, vat vill you say to Him? How vill you plead your case?" Snowshoe, not one to waste an opportunity, be it diversionary or no, was conducting a revival meeting.

Right after that we slipped into the depths of a ravine, out of sight and earshot of the road. I heard Kit mumble, "Oh, no."

"What?" I hissed back.

"It's worse than mules!"

It was true. The transport provided for us was a pair of scrawny Washoe canaries, otherwise known as donkeys. Hawkins, on the other hand, was mounted on his own horse. He did not need to explain his thinking; between our knotted wrists and the deliberate pace of the critters, we would not be racing away.

We hoisted ourselves up onto the bare backs of our mounts with our feet almost dragging the ground. Up the ravine and out on a ledge Hawkins directed us, then a swing west to bypass Genoa, and we were on our way.

Given a peculiarity of the cold, dry air, Snowshoe's sermon still drifted up to us from time to time. I had no doubt that he would keep the gathering occupied until dawn, at which time we would be well out of harm's way.

I felt good about our departure and relaxed enough to be amused at Kit's complaints. This was only possible, however, because none of us had spotted the figure lurking in the trees, watching our exit.

There was no alarm when we circled through the foothills of the Sierras and rejoined the Old Emigrant Road. Once again I found myself headed upward away from Carson County toward Hope Valley. The weather was gathering cold, and the scent of the wind swirling down from the high country had more than a hint of snow to come. I hoped that our passage would get over before the storm arrived, as I did not have my heavy coat and did not relish camping on the mountainside. Sierra storms can last for days before blowing themselves out, and even early in the season can be dangerous to the unprepared.

Westward and up we went, climbing past five thousand feet of elevation on our way toward a pass that would top eight thousand. A coyote was the only traveler who challenged our right-of-way. Gray and bushy-furred, he darted out into the road ahead just at first light. Mid-highway, he turned and faced us, as if startled to see us there. Then he plunged into the mesquite on the other side and disappeared.

The west fork of the Carson tumbled down beside us at this stretch of the track. Though it was the time of low water, it was still musical, dancing across the rocks and pattering over four-foot high waterfalls. The melody of the creek was loud enough to cover the sound of our passage and make it difficult to talk. "That old brush wolf must not have known we were coming. He should be too canny to run out like that," I observed to Kit, raising my voice so he could hear. Then an unpleasant thought struck me. "Or else he was already running from something when he met up with us."

I turned on the donkey's back to pass this worry on to Hawkins. He ignored me.

"That place up ahead, beside the big redwood cedar," I said, "where the trail narrows. It would be a great spot for an ambush."

"Turn around," Hawkins growled, turning up his collar and hunching down inside his wool jacket. "Don't bother playing games with me, Thornton. Nobody is out here but us."

I shrugged and swung back around, but I also kicked the donkey in the flanks and nudged him up closer to Kit. "The leaves look deep on the downhill side," I observed. "Nice and soft."

"Get back there," Hawkins scolded. "Quit talking."

The next bend in the trail was around a boulder the size and shape of a wagon. When the turn was passed, the road was lined up directly with the shoulder of mountain guarded by the cedar.

As soon as Kit turned the corner there was a flash from the hillside near the big tree, and then the boom of a rifle reached us. Kit's donkey reared and screamed, top-pling over on the trail. My brother had not needed my advice because the sudden plunge of his mount had tossed him into the heap of alder leaves. I joined him there myself a second later. My own animal clattered off down the trail.

Another shot boomed, striking the boulder and send-ing a cascade of sparks and rock slivers into the night. Kit and I were not in a good spot, with the lip of the trail barely high enough to cover our heads. Hawkins was in a better position, having the bulk of the stone slab to hide behind. He had his shotgun out, but it was of little use at such a distance.

"This is Deputy Hawkins," he yelled. I guess he was trying to impress our attackers with his authority. "Stop shooting at once."

The words of reply were surprising. "You are sur-rounded by the Thornton gang. Let our chief and his brother go!"

Hawkins swung that cannon to cover us! There is nothing that looks any bigger than the business end of a twelve-gauge from a half dozen feet away! "Don't believe it," I urged. "Whoever is out there wants us dead and maybe you too."

It was all completely clear to me what was up. If Hawkins got away alive, then he would spread the word that he had been jumped by the Thornton gang. After that, no one would care if Kit and I were never seen again. And if Hawkins were slaughtered, too, well, someone would let it be known that the Thorntons had done it, and the result would be the same.

"Give me your Colt," I said.

"Not a chance," Hawkins snarled. "Don't move an inch, or by heaven I'll kill you where you lay and take my chances with your gang."

It came to me that there could not be many men up on the ridge. If they really had us surrounded we would have been cut to pieces already. There could not be more than one or two gunmen.

Another probing round was fired, parting the grass near Kit's head. "You see that?" I spat. "He's aiming for us."

Hawkins ignored me. "If you want 'em," he yelled, "come and get 'em!"

I bunched up in the leaves like I was trying to make myself as small as possible, which was actually a good idea. But my other thought was to reach my boot top and catch the butt end of Kit's knife. My fingers inched downward slow. All the while I was praying that Hawkins would stay focused on the rifleman. In the increasing daylight, even a quick look my direction would give my labor away.

Hawkins decided he might as well make the other party keep his head down, so he blazed away with the coach gun. At such extreme range the shot only rattled in the branches and knocked down some needles, but it would put the gunman on notice.

Unfortunately, the unknown out on the hill was really after us. The next two shots thumped into the body of the donkey where it lay in the road. Any minute now there would be enough light for the shooter to pick out the outlines of our heads from the brush covering, and then we would be up the flume.

Firing again, Hawkins let fly with both barrels, then jumped up and ran around the side of the boulder. I do not know if he was beginning to believe me or not, but he quit watching us so closely. He was trying to outflank the man on the ridge.

Quick as Hawkins moved, I pulled the knife, jammed it handle-first in between two rocks, and started sawing away at my prisoner bracelets. The leather straps parted in a wink, and I hollered to Kit, "Here, catch." I tossed the knife in a gentle arc to land close beside him.

The morning sun beaming into the east-facing canyon caught on the blade. It sparkled in the light and the flash of movement drew a shot from the hillside.

"I'm hit!" Kit yelled. "John, I'm hit!"

I belly-crawled over to him, which caused a bullet to come my way, smacking into a pinecone bare inches from where my head had been. Ripping off his jacket, I found that Kit was struck in the arm. The bullet had gone clear through, but did not seem to have busted the bone. He was losing blood, so I yanked off the bandanna from around my neck and tied it in place over the wound using the rawhide strings which had lately bound my hands. I also retrieved the knife.

"Thornton," Hawkins yelled from the other side of the boulder. "Take my horse and ride. Get out of here."

So he was a believer at last. It did not set well with me to leave him so, shotgun against rifle, but I had no gun at all, and Kit needed help. If we got away clean, I did not think that Hawkins would still be a target for no reason. Right or wrong, I made up my mind to go.

I waited till Hawkins had reloaded both barrels. The bushwhacker must have known something was up because his next shot came from a different angle and went square through Kit's coat where it lay on the pile of leaves.

Hawkins hammered away, and I grabbed up Kit and tossed him over my shoulder. My sudden heave on his injured arm must have pained him considerable, because he gave a groan and went limp. Then I was running for the horse back in the brush beside the stream.

CHAPTER 15

That roan of Hawkins's was not big, but he was young and sturdy. He set off back down the trail at a fair pace, despite the double load he carried. We drew another shot as we passed the boulder. The rock slivers that peppered my back and the flank of the horse pushed him to greater speed to escape the terrible biting critters.

Fast as we rounded the first bend in the trail, I drew rein and cut the roan sharp toward the creek. Just because only one man had been shooting at us did not mean that he did not have confederates waiting below to cut off our escape. Going directly back on the road was almost certain to lead us into more gunplay.

I was in a fair way perplexed about where to go really. Back to Genoa was not an option. Snowshoe's cabin was not far, but not defensible and would not serve Kit's need. The only choice remaining seemed to be the sawmill. I knew that Major Frey would locate us there. My only hope was that the news of our deliverance would be slow in reaching him. If I had time to get back to the mill and fort up with a repeating rifle, perhaps there was still a chance. Maybe we could hold out till Hawkins and a marshall showed up. Between Maria's testimony about how Kit found Bald Hornet and the attempted ambush, our innocence was in a fair way proved.

So putting all this together in my mind, we forded the Carson, and I put the roan at the bank on the far side. It was a steep place and precious little footing. The horse stumbled when his foot slipped on some moss, and Kit and I almost ended up in the river.

We climbed out of the canyon on a zigzag path, taking advantage of every little bit of deer trail. The rifle fire continued from behind us, answered by the roar of Hawkins's shotgun. The higher we rose on that incline, the more sheer it became. I forced myself to think that it was only five feet to the ground from the horse's back; otherwise I would have felt every inch of the two hundred feet down to the stream.

Just above us was a place where the grade leveled out. I was concerned that we might expose ourselves to gunshots when we popped out high up on the ridge like that, so I looked around for a solution. The lip of the precipice was thick with elderberry brush. I gave the roan his head, praying that he would be sensible about finding a way through the tangle. He put his ears back and plowed straight forward into the densest part of the thicket.

Once inside, it was like being in a cave of brush. I could not see out but then neither could anyone see us. Then, near at hand, I heard another horse whinny. It could be where the sharpshooter had tied his mount, or it could be his accomplice waiting to catch us unawares.

Even without a gun there was no help for it. I had to scout ahead on foot to see what we were riding into. I slipped off the roan and fastened it in the elderberry scrub. I looped Kit's still-bound hands over the horn and once more pulled the knife from my boot. I bent low to the ground. Parting the undergrowth with the tip of the blade, I peeked out.

Twenty-five feet away was a saddled horse, and he was looking right at me. Luckily for me, his rider was not so canny. A dozen feet beyond the animal, a man stood with his back to me. He was staring up the canyon toward the sounds of battle. He was armed, but held the rifle with its butt resting on the ground as if he were only a spectator.

Using the bulk of the horse as a cover, I slipped out of the brush and rushed him. He turned at the sound of my running steps, but long before he could bring the weapon up, I was on him. The next second, I was kneeling on his chest with the knife pressed against his throat. It was young Lawrence Frey.

"Don't kill me, Mister Thornton," he blurted.

"What are you up here to do to us?" I snarled.

"Honest, I didn't want anybody to get shot," he pleaded. "It was just to recapture you."

"Who's with you?" I demanded.

"Only Mister Thick."

"Who else?" I snapped, leaning down on the knife a fraction.

Young Frey's eyes bulged. "No one else, I swear it. The Major and King . . ." He stopped, afraid of me and yet fearful of his father's wrath at the same time.

"What about them?" I growled, giving him no pity. Was there another ambush? Were they on the way to join the trap even as I delayed?

"They're going to the sawmill."

My blood chilled in that instant. Maria, George, and the baby at the mercy of those two. "What do they want there?" I asked, shaking the boy's shoulders. "What are they going to do?"

"Nothing," he said, clasping his hands together to beg me not to cut his throat. "Nothing! They just want to keep Missus Thornton from going to town to tell what she knows . . ."

"About the horse," I concluded for him. "Kit was framed."

He nodded miserably.

"Get up," I ordered, yanking him to his feet.

"What are you gonna do to me?"

"Nothing unless you give me any trouble," I warned. "I just figure you may come in handy, so I'm taking you with me."

Lawrence was so frightened that I did not even need to encourage him with the knife. He acted more than willing to be obedient and was soon bound by the arms and tied to the horn.

It was just after sunup when Maria was awakened by the clanking of trace chains and the groan of wagon wheels. Wrapping a blanket around her, she peered out the window into the pale, yellow, early light to see Angie Frey climb down from the wagon while two lathered horses stood with heads bowed at the rail.

No need for Angie to tie them off. The worn-out animals would not move a step unless urged by the whip. It seemed that Angie Frey had disregarded Snowshoe's orders to stay put on the Thompson ranch until morning. Instead, the young lady had finished her supper, allowed the team of horses only three hours in the stall, then had hitched them to the wagon and driven all night over perilous roads to reach the sawmill.

"Missus Thornton!" Angie clambered up the steps and pounded on the door. "Wake up, ma'am! There is trouble in Genoa. You are needed in town."

Knowing that the girl was a close relative of Major Frey caused Maria to hesitate before she opened the door. It came to her mind that those men who wanted to take over the sawmill might well use another female to make Maria lower her guard.

Angie rapped hard on the door. "Missus Thornton! Kit and John are in difficulty! Ma'am? Please open the door! I must have a word with you!"

From his cot, George whispered, "Could be a trick, Mother. Shall I get the gun?"

Maria hushed him with a wave of her hand.

Angie tried once more. "They say Kit shot Si Denton, then rode away on a stolen horse. A big yellow horse it was. They mean to hang him and John Thornton too. Kit says you'll know he didn't steal it. He says you and George can testify that he found the horse . . ."

Believing the girl at last, Maria hurried to throw open the door and let her in.

"Si Denton has been shot?"

"Yes, ma'am." The girl was trembling all over. "Killed stone dead he is! And everything has gone sour."

"Well, girl, you look all together done up."

"I am."

"Come in then, and have a cup of tea. Tell me the news."

Pale, cold to the bone, and exhausted, Angie crumpled into a chair. Near hysterical from weariness and terror, she prattled on about Snowshoe Thompson taking off for Genoa to save Kit and John from a lynching. Then she went on a while about the terrible crowd that had gathered outside the jailhouse. She finished her tale with the story of the trip over the mountain with nothing but starlight to light the way.

Maria stoked the fire in the stove and made the girl sit near to it. She set a kettle of water on to boil and made blackberry tea. The girl's hands were so cold she could not take the cup when Maria gave it to her. Clearly Angie was not a shill sent to lead Maria astray.

"Why, Miss Frey, your hands are ice." Maria rubbed the girl's red, swollen fingers between her own.

With this simple act of kindness Angie began to weep and laid her head against Maria's shoulder. "Oh Missus Thornton! If we're not on our way again soon they'll hang Kit and John for certain!"

Maria instructed George to get his trousers on and go see to the livestock. The boy obeyed, reluctant to miss the rest of the story.

Stroking Angie's head, Maria proclaimed, "Mister Thompson will not allow Kit and John to be lynched. Even the worst of the bad men respect him. They will not cross Snowshoe Thompson. You need to rest a while. Your team is spent."

"You don't understand, Missus Thornton! They believe Kit shot Si Denton! You and your son are the only ones who can testify about the getaway horse!"

It was plain that it would be hours before they could leave for Genoa. Maria looked out the window at the horses. White flecks of lather covered them, and foam dripped from their tongues. They were overheated even in the bitter cold of the morning. Steam rose from their hides.

George glanced up and caught his mother's concerned look as he unhooked the harness. Giving his head a broad shake, he indicated that he had never seen animals so near to collapse as these.

Maria opened the door a crack and called to George. "Don't let them near water until they're cooled down, George. A drink will kill them."

With a curt nod of agreement, George led the animals from the traces and began to walk them slowly. "They're near to dead, Mother," he said grimly. "This bay is lame in the right foreleg. He had a stone wedged between the shoe and the frog. I got it out, but his hoof is bruised. The mare is in better shape. She could take us down the mountain. But there's not much left in either of them."

"Keep them on their feet if you can, son."

From the crib, Maddy whimpered and began to awaken. Maria closed the door, gathered up the baby, then turned to ask Angie, "Miss Frey, how long has it been since you . . ."

But Angie Frey was asleep sitting upright in the chair. Her head nodded forward. Strands of damp hair fell around her face. The half-empty teacup balanced precariously on her lap.

"Poor little thing. You've nearly killed yourself as well as your horses getting here." Maria, holding Maddy to her shoulder, took the cup, roused Angie, and guided her to the bed. The girl tried to protest that time was too short for rest, but she lapsed into a deep sleep even before Maria covered her with the quilt.

Maria knew the bay gelding was a goner from the first moment she laid eyes on it. There was nothing George could do to stop it. The animal dropped into the dust, rolled, twisted a gut, and was dead within an hour.

Angie Frey slept without stirring even after George finished his duties and entered the house with a slam of the door.

"Well, that's that," George said grimly, sitting down to eat a bowl of grits. "I think the mare will live, but she ain't pulling any wagon down to Genoa." He jerked his thumb at Angie on the bed. "She might as well stayed at Snowshoe Thompson's and slept for all the good her night ride has done. One horse is dead, the other useless. . . . And look at her. Is she still breathing?"

"Snowshoe will send someone to see to us when we don't show up in Genoa." Maria took a seat across from her son.

"Uncle John and Kit will be killed by then."

Maria did not reply for a time. She had no way of knowing that Kit and I were riding for our lives at that very moment, and yet she sensed that we were in a bad way.

"George, we're stuck in this cabin, and there's no resurrection for that horse out there. The Lord will fight for Kit and John if we cannot."

"If I was in Genoa I'd fight the whole territory."

Maria inclined her head toward Angie and said solemnly, "The Almighty never wears out. That being the case . . . since we have a dead horse in the yard and we're stuck right where we are . . . I shall pray on the matter and leave it where I must!"

This seemed to satisfy her own mind that Kit and I

were in good hands. (I was having grave doubts at that moment.)

George clenched his fist and gazed down at the muscle on his toothpick arm. "I'm gonna pray I meet up with some of those . . . like Bernard King and Rough Elliott! For what they done to Pa and Samson! When I'm grown . . ."

Maria rose suddenly, signaling the end of the discussion. "Have you chores to do? Have you chopped your kindling?"

"No, ma'am. You know I haven't because of the horses . . ."

"Get to it."

George did not have time to throw his coat on before one portion of his wish was answered. The clatter of hooves put a light in Maria's eyes. "There! You see, George? Mister Thompson has sent someone to fetch us back to Genoa."

Rushing to the door, she threw it open just as Bernard King leapt from his saddle and bounded onto the porch. Maria gave a holler at the sight of the villain. With a rough shove, he pushed Maria back into the cabin and followed, snatching the shotgun from its place beside the door, and then seizing the Volcanic repeater from the wall.

George charged him. King grabbed him up by his trousers and hung him on the gunrack by his belt.

"Well, well, well!" King strutted over to the bed. "Lookie who is here! Indeed! Will you look at this!" He was grinning as he turned to the open doorway. Major Frey strode in.

George called him for the skunk he was and struggled to free himself from the gun peg.

"Let him down," Maria demanded as Frey patted George too hard on the cheek.

George spat on the Major and received a blow in return. Maria attempted to help her son and was pushed hard onto the floor.

"Mother!" George cried and got slapped again, a ringing blow that bloodied his nose and left him limp and stupefied.

When Maria attempted to defend him she was pushed down again and commanded to stay where she was or George would pay for it. King waved the rifle over Angie. "Look here, Major! It's your niece!"

The Major cussed the girl and said he would have her sent back to the orphan home for what she had done. King shook Angie, but Angie could not awaken.

Major Frey towered over her. "My dear niece repays my kindness by stealing my wagon and driving one of my best horses to death. I'll have to take her transgressions out of her hide."

"What do you want with us, Major?" Maria attempted to push herself upright. King kicked her arm out from under her, then stepped down on her wrist, pinning her to the floor.

"What will we do with this lady?" King had not forgotten his humiliation at Maria's hands.

"Why, Mister King. We will just keep her company for a while. It would be no good at all if she were to show up in Genoa as Snowshoe said she would. She might well rouse the good citizens to pity . . ."

"Pity!" Maria gasped. "Only the truth will serve justice! You know Kit did not steal that horse or shoot Constable Denton . . ."

King pushed down harder with his boot against her forearm until she cried out with pain. "Somebody's got to die for bushwhacking Si Denton. It don't matter to the law-abiding citizens who gets hung as long as their appetite for justice is satisfied."

Frey rubbed his whiskers thoughtfully. "You see, Missus Thornton, we cannot have you keep the Vigilance Committee from doing its duty!" He pantomimed the hangman's noose around his neck and gave a strangled cry. "Kit and John Thornton will soon be on their way to the hereafter, and then Missus Thornton may go free. She may go wherever she likes as long as it is nowhere in my territory."

When a couple of hours had passed, Angie was awake but still groggy and frightened besides. The three hostages formed a row of downcast figures seated on the cot. George was still spoiling for a fight, but his mother convinced him that he would endanger the baby if he acted up.

When hoofbeats were heard coming up the road from town, Frey motioned for King to stand guard over the prisoners. "Keep 'em quiet," he ordered the gambler.

The Major opened the door a crack and held the repeating rifle at his side.

An instant later he announced, "It's Rough."

Elliott reported how Hawkins had succeeded in getting Kit and me out from under the noses of the lynch mob. Rough weathered the Major's temper tantrum by explaining how Thick had left in plenty of time to set up an ambush in the Hope Valley narrows. "It'll be the Thornton gang that did it," he said. "However it turns out, they are done for now."

Maria gave a gasp, and King made an elaborate shushing motion as if her dismay was a great and humorous occurrence. Then he asked a question. "I thought we had a guard back of the jail?"

"That's right," the Major agreed. "That crazy Norwegian preacher might gull the crowd, but what happened to Lawrence? Did he fall asleep?"

Elliott grimaced and then replied, "Lawrence came and told me about the escape . . . but he acted like he wanted them to get away."

The Major harumphed and pondered aloud what the younger generation was coming to. "Unreliable," he concluded. "I'll settle with him . . . and you," he said, looking at Angie, "later." Then to Elliott he said, "Rough, I want you out in the sawmill. Get up on the roof where you can keep an eye on things."

CHAPTER 16

Many and troubled were the thoughts in my head. I had planned to seek help for Kit by going to the sawmill. Now it seemed I was riding straight into a bigger problem than before. At least Kit's wound had stopped bleeding. He did not appear as bad off as I had first imagined, only hurting and weak from the blood loss.

My brother was half awake, at least enough to sit up and hang on, and I figured to make better time by having him ride behind Lawrence Frey. The two of them together just barely weighed as much as me, and we moved out smartly.

It felt good to have a rifle in my hands again. Though I would have preferred my own repeater, the fifty-two caliber Sharps was a solid weapon. There was a pouch of powder and shot and a tin of primers as well.

"Why didn't you shoot?" I asked Lawrence. "From your angle you could have nailed all three of us."

The young man shook his head. It was plain he had no interest in gunplay or killings.

"Who killed Si?" I asked as we rode.

"Rough Elliott," was the not-unexpected reply.

It was a concern to me to know Elliott's whereabouts Of all those who ranged on the side of the Major, Elliott was the most hardened case and the most adept killer. Leaving him unaccounted for made me want to look over my shoulder regular.

I was still searching all around me when we finally arrived at the bluff overlooking the sawmill. There was a sizable lake backed up behind Kit's dam, poised to rush down the flume.

Since I was expecting to find vicious dogs in the front yard, I intended to get in by way of the back. My one advantage was that they were not expecting me. The Major probably figured to hold Maria until he got word that Thick had succeeded in killing Kit and Hawkins and me. Then he would let Maria go . . . I hoped.

The question was, since I did not intend to die to oblige the Major's plans, how could I get Maria and the children free without harm coming to them? Maybe a trade could be arranged?

When I took stock of the situation, it did not look too good for our side. I had a single-shot rifle—accurate, to be sure, with plenty of ammunition, but still only one gun. Kit, though in no immediate danger, was still a worry, since he could not defend himself. Holding Lawrence Frey was a definite ace for this high-stakes game, but how to play him was the question.

On the other side were three big strikes against me, and they were named Maria, George, and Maddy. If any threat were leveled against them, I doubted if I could go through with my plan. If that were not enough, ranged against me were the Major and King. Rough Elliott was out there somewhere, and maybe Thick as well. Shoot, for all I knew, Elliott might be on his way right now with a lynch mob, unconvinced by Snowshoe's preaching.

As the saying is, when the music starts, it's time to dance.

I propped Kit in the shade beside the sizable lake backed up behind the dam above the flume, then, grasping Lawrence by the rope tied to his wrists, I went to the edge of the drop and hollered down. "Major Frey! It's John Thornton, Frey. I've got your son!"

There was no sound and no movement for a time, and then the door of the cook shack creaked open and the Major yelled back. "Let him go, Thornton. I don't want to hurt Maria Thornton or the children."

"Let me see her, Frey," I called. "Let me see that they are all right now."

"Not yet," he countered. "Let me see my son first."

I pulled on Lawrence's leash like dragging an unwilling puppy. He approached the cliff silent and with his head hanging down. I could not read whether he was abashed about being captured or ashamed at his father's business.

"There he is, Frey. Let me have a look at Maria."

"You know, Thornton," the Major countered, making no move toward the cabin door, "the smartest thing you could do right now would be to hightail it out of here. There'll be a posse arriving before long, anxious to hang the killer of Si Denton. And Hawkins too? Did you drygulch him?"

"Give it a rest, Major! Your boy Thick failed. Hawkins knows the truth. There'll be a posse along all right, but they'll be after you, not me."

Frey seemed to study on this a while, and he still did not bring out Maria. A new thought struck me: Was it possible that he did not have them after all? Could she be safe already?

A movement on the roof of the sawmill was all that saved my life. I flung myself down on the ground and dragged Lawrence prone too. I got a mouthful of sand for my trouble, but I missed catching a slug with my teeth. Rough Elliott fired, and a rifle bullet slammed into the post back of where my head had been. The Major's speechifying had just been a play for time to let Elliott get in position. I guess I am a slow learner.

From flat down, I took a steady rest for my weapon and squeezed off a shot of my own. That Sharps bucked and kicked like Kit's mule. The shell tore through the shingles just at Elliott's feet, making him dive for the cover of a gable. "Watch it! He's got a gun!" he yelled, somewhat unnecessarily to my way of thinking. The Sharps was shooting a touch low, so I adjusted the sights accordingly.

The battle was on. Major Frey triggered off a couple

rounds as he ducked back inside the cook shack, but they were both wide and high.

Lawrence seized the opportunity to try and crawl away, but I caught the trailing end of the rope and whipped a couple turns around the flume post. "Where you bound to?" I asked. "You don't want to miss this party."

Elliott had moved to the other side of the gable to change his angle on me. When he fired this time, the bullet hit just in front of my face. I scooted back quick, digging in the pouch for the bullet and powder flask. The Sharps loaded a single round at the breech when you cranked down on a lever, dropping the block and exposing the chamber. I shoved in another fifty-two caliber lead slug, wadding, and powder, and clamped it shut again. Applying a new percussion cap made the weapon ready to fire again.

I waited till Rough Elliott leaned out from behind the gable, and then I let fly. This bullet must have creased his cheek, because I heard him yell and saw his hand fly up to his face before he ducked down again. "Major," he yelled. "This ain't workin'. Let's rush him."

This was bad for me if they carried it out. I could not hope to reload fast enough to hold them both off. What I had going for me was the fact that nobody wants to die, and what they both realized was that if I could not get both, I could surely get one.

"I've got a better idea, Major," I hollered as I reloaded. "Let's work on that trade again—Lawrence for

Maria, George, and Maddy, and you can ride out of here."

There was silence again for a time. I had another worry still: Where was Bernard King? He was no kind of hand with a long gun. Sneaking close for a back shot was more his style.

"All right, Thornton," Major Frey finally replied through the barely cracked door. "You win. I'm bringing Maria out now."

"Call off your dog," I countered. "Get Elliott down off the roof, and keep him where I can see him."

With Elliott beside the mill building, the Major brought Maria outside. She had a bandanna tied over her mouth as a gag. "Let me talk to her," I said, making Lawrence Frey stand up in front of me. The Major untied the cloth. "Are you all right?" I asked. Maria nodded. Then I tried to learn all I could without giving too much away. "Is everything all right?" I said, leaning on the words and hoping she understood I was asking about the children. She gave a terse nod.

Behind the Major I saw Angie Frey emerge from the cook shack window. She had a bundle in her arms that could only be Maddy. With the attention of both Elliott and the Major fixed on me, they did not see her go, and she disappeared into a side door of the mill building.

"What do you say, Thornton? Is it a deal?"

From back of me I heard Kit yell, "John! Look out for King!"

There was no time to think. Once more I flung myself

to the ground, just as my prophecy came true: Bernard King fired both barrels of his palm gun from a distance of twenty feet away at what would have been my spine. But what he hit instead was Lawrence Frey. The boy took two bullets in his midsection. He grabbed his belly with both hands and doubled over, then slumped to his knees.

I gave King the benefit of a reply from the Sharps, and no further apart then we were, the slug did not just hit him in the stomach, it tore his middle clear out. King was flung backward, but he was dead long before he ever hit the ground.

"Lawrence!" the Major shrieked, having seen his son go down. "Lawrence!"

The boy struggled to reply. "I didn't tell, Dad," he pleaded in a barely audible voice. "I didn't tell." Then he fell facedown on the ground.

Rough Elliott had not waited to see how the little scene would play out. He was already running for the base of the hill, trying to outflank me. Firing his rifle from the hip as he ran, he forced me to stay down.

I barely had time to spare a glance for Maria. What I saw was the Major shoving her roughly back inside the shack. I guessed he would tie her up again, but with him crazed with grief, I was more frightened for her now than before.

I slithered over to the dropoff and fired downward at Elliott as he ran to the very base of the flume. My shot missed, and he fired back at the same instant. By the worst of unlucky breaks, his bullet hit the muzzle of the Sharps, knocking it out of my hands. Worse still, the barrel shattered. I was weaponless again.

Although he could not see the result of the volley from where he was, it would only be an instant before Elliott figured out what had happened. When I did not return his fire again, he would be all over me.

I looked around for something with which to fight back. A rock, a shovel, anything. Then it struck me—a shovel and a rock! I grabbed up the shovel and tore into the dam holding back the water from the flume. Three sharp, clanging blows had no effect. I stuck the blade of the tool under the boulder at the base of the pile and heaved on the lever with all my weight. Still nothing. Elliott would be gathering himself for a rush soon. I threw myself down on the handle again and the old wood snapped with the force, throwing me to the ground.

Then the boulder moved. A fine spray haloed the rock and pushed it ahead a little, then a little more. The pressure of the rushing water increased as it found the weak spot and forced the gap ever wider. Then suddenly, with the impetus of a fire hose, a gush of unleashed power not only jetted through the opening but rolled the boulder in front of it as well.

There was a rumble and a roar, as if the mountain was suddenly seized in the throes of an avalanche. I got down behind a support pillar again to see if I had been in time.

Elliott had climbed the hillside cautiously, running from boulder to tree stump, fearful that I was laying a trap. How right he was!

He had just arrived at the gap in the wooden conduit when the first of the water reached him. I saw him look up suddenly as a couple of drops fell on his head from what had been a dry channel before.

Then his countenance showed amazement as the noise reached him. He looked so startled you could have knocked his eyes out of his head without touching the rest of his face! The next second that boulder, propelled by tons of water dropping eighty feet, hit him in the chest and bowled him over. He disappeared from view.

Things had evened up some. King was dead, and so was Elliott, or at least incapacitated for the time. It was me against Frey, and I was ready.

The Major had to still be holed up inside the cook shack. At least he had not rejoined the fight. I scampered down the hillside, slipping and sliding. At the bottom lay Rough Elliott. He was laying clutching that rock to his chest like it was a pillow. I spared him little regard, apart from picking up the rifle he had been carrying. It was my own Volcanic, and the magazine was fully loaded.

"Frey," I yelled from the cover of the mill race. "King is dead. So is your son. So is Elliott. It's all over, Major. Give yourself up."

The door opened again and Frey emerged, but he was holding his pistol against Maria's head. "Come out," he hissed, "unless you want her to die. You are not going to outlive my son, unless at the expense of her life."

"You can't mean it, Major," I responded. "You know you can't hurt a woman and rest easy. There'll be no place in the world that will shelter you if you harm her." Now it was my turn to play for time.

Major Frey pressed the muzzle of the revolver into Maria's ear. "I mean it, Thornton," he wailed. "Get out here and take what's coming to you, or I swear I'll kill her."

"Don't come out, John!" Maria called. "Save yourself."

"Shut up!" the Major ordered, and he swiped Maria across the back of the head with the pistol.

It made me so mad I stood straight up.

It was then that George, who had torn up the floorboards of the cabin, came dashing out from under the porch. He had an ax handle in his paws and he swung it with all the force of his young life, right at the back of the Major's knees. "Don't hurt my mother!" George screamed.

Major Frey's aim was caught in an arc between me, Maria, and the boy and pointing at nothing when the club knocked the props out from under him. The gun went off, shooting into the ground at his feet. Maria broke free of his grip, and George raised his sights a touch and clobbered the Major's gun hand, knocking the pistol spinning away.

After one futile grab for the boy's hair, the Major

ducked behind the cook shack and out of sight before I could fire another shot.

Maria and George ran to my arms. I held them for only a moment. Though I wanted the moment to last forever, right then was not the time. "He's still a rattler," I warned. "As long as he's loose, nobody is safe."

Maria was already past thinking about Major Frey. She bent down and cuddled George, who struggled and made protesting sounds. Then a new worry came to her. "Maddy! She's with Angie, John. Where can they have gone?"

"It's all right, Maria," I said. "I saw her sneak out and run to the mill . . ." The mill! My words trailed away with the recognition that the mill was the direction the Major had taken. "Go in the shack, and bar the door," I said, hurrying them along. "Don't open up unless it's me or someone you trust. And don't worry. I'll go get 'em."

I heard Angie screaming before I ever got inside the mill. "Keep back, Uncle," she was yelling. "Keep away from us."

Levering in another shell I called out, "Give up, Frey!" A sawhorse tumbled down from the floor above, barely missing my head. I was afraid to shoot, because in the dusty and dim interior of the building, I could not be certain I would not hit Angie or Maddy.

I believe that Major Frey was genuinely crazy by then. He could not be reasoned with because he was not sane. He was out for revenge, and nothing, not even my rifle, would easily deter him.

The sawdust on the floor stilled the sound of my footsteps, but then it did the same for the Major. By passing the main stairs, I crept to one end of the building and climbed a ladder to the second floor. The sound of running feet came to me from one floor higher yet. I could make out Angie running along a catwalk. She was still carrying the baby. Reasoning that Major Frey was chasing her, I started toward them to cut him off.

A sixty-pound block-and-tackle swung out of the gloom and smashed into my side. I barely had time to drop my shoulder and meet the blow, or it would have busted my ribs. As it was, the impact numbed my right arm. I switched the Volcanic to the other side, but I was awkward at best shooting left-handed.

Knowing that Angie was safely up another level, I triggered off a shot in the direction of the pulley's travel, but hit nothing. Worse, the muzzle flash blinded me. As I groped along the catwalk, holding the rifle before me as if it were a sightless man's cane, I almost walked right into my death.

Frey waited until I was directly under the giant sawblade suspended from the works overhead, then he threw the lever of the jacking gear. I had only a flash of movement to warn me as the blade descended. Even unpowered as it was, its weight alone, and the dagger-like teeth, would have cut me in two if it had connected. Instead of my flesh, the cutting edge hit the gunbarrel of the repeater, sending it spinning down to the bottom of the mill. Then the sawblade hung in the void, swaying back and forth and leering like a hideously fanged mouth.

Then he was on me. Major Frey jumped at me out of the darkness. His hands closed around my neck and I was little able to fight back after the blow to my shoulder. We rolled over and over on the catwalk. He was snarling and biting, no longer even human in his actions but purely an animal fighting out of hatred.

He put his forearm across my throat, leaning down and pummeling me about the face with his fists. Feeling my consciousness slipping away, I fumbled with my boot top, looking for the hilt of the knife.

I had only gotten it half drawn when the Major saw what I was about. With a shout of triumph, he released his grip with one hand and seized the knife, flourishing it over my face.

But the change in position was what I needed to give me some leverage. I kicked up hard with both legs, catching Frey off-balance. His body lurched toward the edge of the sawpit, his hands scrambling frantically for purchase on the planks. His fingers twined in my hair as he tried to stop himself from flying forward, but his momentum was too great.

Hurtling into the air, a handful of my pelt clutched between his hands, Major Frey shot over the edge of the walkway. A moment later there was a terrible scream, then silence. I looked over the edge of the catwalk.

Frey hung in midair, swinging back and forth on the great circular cutter. He was impaled on its teeth and quite dead before I got to him.

When I shepherded Angie and the baby past the gruesome sight and out into daylight again, the yard was filled with people. Snowshoe Thompson had arrived, and with him was Paul Hawkins and Raycraft and others from town.

"Where's Frey?" Hawkins asked.

"Dead," I said quietly. "King and Elliott too. Also young Lawrence, shot by King when he was aiming for me."

Hawkins shook his head sadly. "What a terrible price the Major paid for his greed," he said.

"Do you know it all now?" I asked.

Hawkins nodded. "Snowshoe and I pieced it together. We confronted Lute Olds, who was selling meat from the stolen cattle. He's in jail now. Thick got away, but I've already sent word to Placerville. We'll get him."

Maria, holding Maddy in her arms, and clasped around the waist by her son, joined us. "Did King really own the sawmill?"

Snowshoe Thompson shook his bearded visage. "He choost thought he could scare you off."

"Then perhaps we can restore it and put it back to work?"

"You don't know the half of it," Hawkins added. "There was reward money up for Edwards that belongs to you, John. And an even bigger sum was offered by Gordier's relatives for his killer . . . who was Rough Elliott. That money rightly belongs to you too. You and Kit."

"Kit!" I said, slapping myself on the forehead. "I clean forgot him. I left him lying wounded at the head of the flume."

"I'll go get him," Hawkins volunteered. "It's the least I can do after almost getting him hanged."

I shook my head. "It's all right," I said. "You better see to Frey's body. I'll go take care of Kit."

Struggling with stiffness that seemed to be settling in over my whole body I labored back up the precipice to where my baby brother still sat with his back against a tree.

"'Bout time," he scolded. "I was beginning to think you got yourself killed."

"Not me," I disagreed. "But you look enough like death still that I'll bet Angie Frey will need a month to nurse you back to health."

Kit was indeed staring over my shoulder as if he saw the grim reaper approaching. Then he yelled, "Look out!"

A battered and blood-stained Rough Elliott rose up behind me. Over his head he held a rock with which he intended to bash out my brains.

I caught his arms just before he could throw it. The

two of us, both abused almost to the point of collapse, struggled to keep the boulder aloft.

We staggered together toward the brink of the cliff. I made the mistake of looking down and felt the world spin beneath me, all eighty feet of drop. "If I go, I'm taking you with me," Elliott growled. I believed him.

There was just one chance. If I could use the momentum in the weight of the stone . . .

We danced a drunken waltz of death there on the brink, and then, just as Elliott felt me sway and gave a yelp of victory, I sprang for the flume. The over-balanced motion pushed me into the vee-shaped channel. With the water now flowing, I shot like a log down toward the bottom, fetching up through the gap in the structure and landing hard on my injured shoulder. But the water and the mud cushioned my descent, leaving me only stunned.

Elliott was not so lucky. Without me to support his weight, he also fell toward the flume, but he did not make it. He tumbled over the edge of the bluff and bounced once on the rocks at the bottom. This time he was well and truly dead.

EPILOGUE

Wise way beyond his years, George asked me why his daddy had not yelled out the name of his abductor, since he must have recognized the Major's voice. I replied that no matter his faults, my brother Lucky had cared for his family and knew such knowledge would endanger their lives. Thinking on that fact helped George some; Maria too.

Kit and Angie got hitched on the same spring day as Maria and me.

In a year's time Genoa doubled in size. Travel from the East grew more and more regular, and Carson Valley attracted folks eager to ranch and lead civilized lives. The business of the sawmill boomed, and no more was heard of The Committee.

Then silver was discovered in the mines of Virginia City—hundreds of miles of tunnels and shafts, all needing to be propped up with square-set timbers, of which Thornton Lumber was the proud supplier.

We debated long and hard about the company name. Kit was square in favor of Thornton Brothers, but that name would not have told the whole story for long. Soon enough it should have been Thornton Brothers, Sons, and Nephew, and even George allowed that was way too cumbersome.

HISTORICAL NOTE

The late 1850s were a time of tremendous upheaval across North America. Bloody struggles in Kansas and Missouri spelled out the confrontation that would set the United States on the inescapable path toward civil war.

The far West was also in turmoil. By 1858, the early placer deposits that had sparked the Gold Rush of '49 had long since given out; the time when a lone man could make a fortune from the streams of the Sierra was gone. Many who could not find the expected easy pickings in a gold pan refused to go back to dreary occupations in the East. Some settled down to ranching and raising families . . . some took up revolvers and masks.

When arson and looting in San Francisco were ignored by corrupt officials, it led to the organization of vigilante groups. But all too often, vigilantism produced "lynch law" and private vendettas in the name of justice.

Genoa's brush with "The Committee" is just a small reflection of what happened throughout the West in the middle decade of the nineteenth century. Snowshoe Thompson saw it all and became a sort of one-man CNN of his day.

ABOUT THE AUTHOR

Brock Thoene, author of *The Legend of Storey County*, has coauthored with his wife, Bodie, a number of best-sellers including *Shiloh Autumn*, *The Twilight of Courage*, *The Saga of the Sierras Series*, *The Zion Chronicles Series*, *The Zion Covenant Series*, and *The Shiloh Legacy Series*. The Thoenes have won seven ECPA Gold Medallion Awards for fiction. They live near Lake Tahoe, Nevada.